THE DARK GATEWAY

In a lonely corner of Wales, an ancient castle quivers with evil as menacing powers return from beyond . . . The family living on the hillside farm with their daughter, Nora, has a stranger coming to live with them. But he's not what he seems — he will not fulfil Nora's hopes of romance . . . As the powers of darkness approach, the human race is in danger and the earth itself is at stake. In this frightened community, who will oppose the invaders?

JOHN BURKE

THE DARK GATEWAY

Complete and Unabridged

LINFORD
Leicester

First published in Great Britain

First Linford Edition
published 2011

British Library CIP Data

Burke, John Frederick, *1922* –
   The dark gateway. - -
   (Linford mystery library)
   1. Strangers- -Wales- -Fiction.
   2. Suspense fiction.
   3. Large type books.
   I. Title II. Series
   823.9′14–dc22

ISBN 978–1–4448–0924–4

Published by
F. A. Thorpe (Publishing)
Anstey, Leicestershire

Set by Words & Graphics Ltd.
Anstey, Leicestershire
Printed and bound in Great Britain by
T. J. International Ltd., Padstow, Cornwall

This book is printed on acid-free paper

1

She awoke in the cold, dim light of morning. The temperature had, she knew at once, fallen below freezing point during the night, but she was conscious of perspiration damp on her forehead. There had been a dream ... Still on the borderland of sleep, she tried to look back into the country she had left, to catch a glimpse of what had frightened her, but the memory was fading, leaving only a feeling of horror dragging at her mind, like the ebbing tide sucking at the shore.

She turned over to look at the window, and saw that the slope of the hill rising to the castle was still white with snow. The ruins themselves were partly submerged in the whiteness, but here and there a black and twisted fang thrust up towards the flushed sky.

The dream — she remembered suddenly — a remembrance like an echo that hollowly sounded once and faded quickly

— had been about the castle. The ruins of the old Welsh stronghold, so familiar a sight from any of the windows at the back of the farmhouse, had in some way been bound up with her terror. It was useless trying to recall the details: dreams that were vivid and possessive during the night hours lingered only as uneasy sensations when daylight came, sensations that soon died away. In any case, she preferred to forget. It would be better. Without knowing exactly what it was that had troubled her, she hoped fervently that it would not come again.

The whole thing had been Simon's fault. He had been talking so wildly and irrationally the previous evening, with an almost fanatical gleam in his eye. She could still hear ringing in her ears the words that had given rise to her nightmare.

'If you let this man come down and stay here, there'll be great harm done. I'm not crazy: I'm serious. You must believe me. I can't tell you the whole story right now, but you must listen to me, believe me . . . This house is more than just a house. And those ruins — that's where the gateway is, and it ought not to be opened yet. This isn't the time . . . '

When they asked him what he was talking about, and tried to make sense out of his ramblings, he repeated grimly: 'The time hasn't come. It'll be too risky. You mustn't let him take the risk; you mustn't let that man stay here.'

Later, he had talked in a more level tone, but the fact that he was unable or unwilling to name what it was that he feared did not help to make his meaning any clearer. Whatever it may have been that prompted his insistence on the necessity for keeping Mr. Jonathan away, his words had certainly had unpleasant consequences for Nora.

She got out of bed, shivering as her feet touched the carpet, and unwilling to move out on to the cold boards that intervened between the edge of the carpet and her dressing-table. Mother was already up: the usual bumping noises were rising from the kitchen, and by the time Nora was ready to go downstairs she heard the rasp and scrape of ashes being shovelled into a bucket.

The kitchen was cold when she went in, and her feet rang on the stone floor. Until the fire took hold, the room seemed strangely empty, and she kept herself warm by following a well-established routine of early morning tasks, scarcely exchanging a word with her mother. They worked with their mouths shut, as though to keep out the probing, unrelenting chill of the atmosphere. In the fireplace, unenthusiastic tongues of flame licked tentatively around the wood.

'What a bitter morning,' said Nora. She was still upset by her dream, and felt irritable. 'If only we could lie in bed until it got warm, and get up when we felt like it!'

'In that case we'd lie there all day,' said her mother. 'It won't get much warmer today.' She swung the huge kettle towards the tap. 'I expect we'll have more snow.'

Nora groaned. There were times when she hated the sight and smell of this kitchen, all the jobs that had to be done there, and the knowledge that outside was the farmyard, soon to be trampled into

4

brown slush as the day's work went on. To escape from all this . . .

She noticed that the lamp was still burning, and turned it out.

Her mother said: 'Best give your father a shout. We're late this morning.'

Nora went upstairs and knocked on the doors of her father's and brother's rooms. When she came down, the kitchen seemed warmer and more cheerful.

'You were very rude to Simon last night,' said her mother suddenly.

'Rude, was I? It was all I could do to sit and listen to him talking so much nonsense. He goes on and on for so long, but you never get any idea of what he's supposed to be talking about.'

'He's a nice boy. You used to like him.'

'Just because I used to like him doesn't mean that — oh, Mum, you know he's impossible. All he ever thinks of is the castle and those books. Honestly, I can't even look up the hill now without thinking of all the stuff he talks about — and last night I was dreaming about it.'

'Perhaps he does read too much,' her

mother conceded. 'Too much studyin' all the time.'

'It's all he comes here for,' said Nora. 'Those awful books . . . I wish Dad would stop him coming.'

'Your dad said he should come whenever he wanted to, isn't it? He used to come in to read those books before you were ever interested in him.'

She smiled. The truth of this remark was no comfort to Nora. She warmed her hands by the swelling fire, then went into the parlour and stood aggressively in front of the book-case. It looked very imposing, with its orderly shelves of beautifully-bound volumes — volumes that no-one would want to read, she thought angrily, except Simon. She wondered what queer kink in his mind made him interested in these dull things. Many were in French or Latin, and one or two in languages she did not recognise. The few in English had seemed promising at first: she had been fascinated by the strange illustrations, and the detailed accounts of witchcraft trials and strange practices in remote parts of the country in days long past had looked exciting . . . at first. But when Nora had settled down to read any of the books, she found that she became sleepy. The words failed to mean anything. It was as though they pushed her gently away and settled back in their places to await another, more understanding reader. Perhaps there were terrible things to be discovered, if one read on far enough. But that was Simon again, putting ideas into her head. Nora wished her father would get rid of the books.

Her reflection moved gently and ethereally in the glass, wavering like a ghost over the books. There was no colour in it: the dark hair that blazed defiant auburn when the light caught it was nothing now but a darker shadow, and for once her features looked pale and elusive; Nora had always been glad that her eyebrows did not look as pale and thin as the eyebrows of so many red-haired people seem, and that her skin did not freckle easily — except, she admitted unwillingly, in the corners of her eyes and sporadically down the sides of her nose. The solemn wraith in the glass stared

7

back at her. Overhead, she could hear the sound of her brother moving reluctantly about. She gave the bookcase one last venomous glare, seeing her grimacing reflection and realising how silly she was being. She went back into the kitchen. The kettle was beginning to sing.

'Why don't we get rid of those old books?' she said after a few minutes.

Her mother, leaning over the fire, said: 'Where would we get rid of them?'

'Burn them.'

'Your dad would never let us burn them. He says they're worth a lot of money. He wants us to keep them until he knows what they *are* worth.'

'If anything.'

'Simon's found them interesting enough.' She smiled as she spooned tea into the pot. 'Is that why — ?'

'No, mother, it's not. I just think it's silly to clutter up the house with old books. We ought to sell them, or give them to the chapel for the next jumble sale.'

'I don't think they'd be right for chapel jumble sale,' said her mother dryly.

'Well, why not try and find out what they're worth? I think Dad just likes to sit and watch the lamplight on the bindings.'

Her mother shrugged. For some reason her husband was attracted to the books that the previous owner had left behind, though she had never seen him reading one. Men had whims: Rhys Morris had plenty of them, and you could do nothing but accept them.

'If he wants to find out, he'll do it in his own good time. Some day — '

'Some day!'

Nora could have choked with disgust. It was always the same. Some day. Some day, someone will mend the front gate, swinging loose on one hinge; some day, someone will see about the hot water system, that has always been queer. Some day . . . it was the old story.

She heard her father coming downstairs. She said: 'Nothing ever gets done in this house.'

'A fine mood you're in this morning, my girl.'

Nora picked up a cup of tea that had been poured out. She walked over to the

9

small side window, looking down the slope. The narrow lane up to the farm was stifled with snow.

'I'm sorry,' she said. 'I had a bad night, and I feel awful. Mother, don't you ever feel that this house is getting you down?'

Her father came in. A cheerful man at most times, he was taciturn and remote in the mornings. He would not waste a word, and there would be no murmur of his deep, characteristic chuckle until breakfast-time. He peered into a cup, added more sugar without tasting the tea, and sat down with a sigh by the table.

Nora stayed by the window, staring out until her eyes ached. To get away from this house; to go somewhere and see things. But what? This was the sort of place from which you did not break away. She knew the girls of her own age in the district, nearly all farmers' daughters, tied down until old age: even those who married usually married farmers, and life was still the same, and there was another family in the district, and the same routine to go through in the house — on and on and on.

She knew that her mother was looking at her. Turning from the window, she said with forced casualness:

'I wonder why Mr. Jonathan wants to come down now? We don't usually get visitors at this time of year.'

Her father got up and opened the door, admitting a knife-edged gust of cold air.

'Better get the buckets from the dairy,' he said gruffly.

Nora put her cup back on the table and went into the dairy, the clean, sterilised smell annoying her by its very familiarity. This was all part of it. On her way back through the kitchen she could not resist glancing once more towards the small window. Her mother said gently:

'No silly ideas, Nora fach. And it's no good lookin' out yet: he won't be here till this afternoon.'

2

The man who ploughed his way up from the village through the snow drifts, heaped up before and around him like fantastically-shaped meringues, was not suitably dressed for the occasion. He was wearing a dark suit, a sober black overcoat and a black hat, and looked as though he had come straight here from some city office. He was carrying a small case that brushed against the snow along the side of the lane, and his trousers were soaked up to the knees.

Nevertheless, he was smiling as he looked up at the farmhouse and the shattered castle beyond. Small, black and incongruous, he stood at the foot of the slope up to the house and looked with apparent equanimity — almost with satisfaction — at the waist-high drifts through which he had yet to fight his way. About him and below, the dazzling, painfully white glaring fields sloped and reeled away, the village itself almost lost in what appeared as an uneven hummock of snow broken only by occasional grey roofs or patches of street that had been cleared.

The man pushed onwards. He was breathing heavily by the time he reached the front gate of the farm, his face an unhealthy colour. He coughed — a hoarse, smoker's cough. It took all his strength to open the small gate, cutting a wide swathe through the white carpet that lay evenly and indiscriminately over the front lawn — its untidiness now hidden — and the gravel path. There were no marks of footsteps up to the front door and the ramshackle porch because no one who knew the family ever used the front door. The house was shaped like a large, grey L, two doors opening from the back into the farmyard. Everyone came and went by means of the door that gave access to the kitchen. The path that led around the side of the house by the once ornamental hedge was overgrown in summer, and was now choked with snow. It was rarely used; only strangers came to the front of the house.

The visitor took his last few steps, glancing around with a smug look of satisfaction, and knocked.

The use of the large brass knocker invariably created confusion throughout the house. Anyone who knocked at the front door must be a stranger, and that, according to Mrs. Morris, meant bad news. She would turn white, clutch her pinafore to dry her hands — even if they were not wet — and say: 'Oh, dear. Now what? And I haven't done my hair neither.' She would tremble and fiddle with her hair . . . even to-day, when she must have known who it would be. In the end it was, as usual, Nora who went to open the door.

'Good afternoon, Mr. Jonathan. We didn't expect — '

'Good afternoon, Miss Morris.'

'We didn't really expect you. We thought the weather would have put you off.'

She pulled the door open wide; it creaked a squeaky protest. Mr. Jonathan entered and stood in the narrow stone passage, holding his case away from his damp legs and grimacing.

'I had no idea how wet I was becoming,' he said, in a precise voice that did not quite eliminate his Liverpool accent.

Nora took his coat, shook it and hung it beside her own. Mr. Jonathan put down his case, then picked it up again.

'Come into the kitchen and dry yourself,' said Nora. 'And perhaps I'd better take your coat and hang it on a chair. If you've brought a change of clothing — '

'I'm afraid I omitted to take that precaution. As it was only for a weekend, you know. Foolish of me, wasn't it?'

Nora was trying to fight down her disappointment. This was what she ought to have expected. If she had not allowed her imagination to dictate to her memory, she would not at this moment be feeling so annoyed. It was her own fault. Since the day that Jonathan had written, asking if he could come down for a weekend, she had been building up the most extravagant hopes. Why should he want to come

15

down in the middle of winter to a place where he had spent one week's holiday in the summer? Without consciously wishing the thoughts to come to her, she had imagined — only imagined, at first — what it would be like if he had been so attracted by her that he had decided to come back and ask her if she would leave the farmhouse, to go with him . . . It was the dream of leaving the house that had attracted her, and at once she was able to find reasons for believing that she might, at last, get away from it. She was surprised to find that her recollections of Mr. Jonathan were vague, but she filled in details and built up quite an attractive picture of him. A middle-aged, understanding sort of man, with a quality all his own. Her youth had appealed to him, and he was coming back. What had started out as a dream became reality. She had almost expected that when she opened the door — well, what had she expected? It was all gone now. Already it was incredible that she should ever have found it hard to thrust such an absurd idea from her mind.

But if he had not come to see her, what could have brought him down on a day like this?

Mr. Jonathan, still clinging to his case, went thankfully towards the fire, greeting Mrs. Morris in his clipped, sibilant voice. She pulled up a chair for him, and he sat down before the leaping flames, the steam from his trousers mingling with the steam from the spout of the perpetually-boiling kettle.

'That's better,' he said, and he put his case on the floor beside the chair.

'A cup of tea, Mr. Jonathan?' said Nora.

'Thank you. Yes, it would be very welcome.'

Mrs. Morris hovered anxiously about him, going 'Tch, tch,' and saying: 'If your clothes — well, with all the damp there is . . . I expect Rhys could find you something.'

'No, really. Very kind of you, but I'll soon be dry. If only I had realised how bad it was going to be — '

'I s'pose it wasn't like this when you left Liverpool?'

'All the snow was trampled into slush days ago. People and traffic, you know. I was quite surprised to see how white and clean everything looked when we left Chester. The further we got into Wales, the thicker it got.'

'You picked a bad time to come down here. We don't get many visitors this time of year.'

'Very good of you to have me — very kind indeed. I don't mind the weather.' He smiled strangely. 'I had to come this weekend. I've found out so many things just lately.'

Nora watched him without seeming to. She was shocked by the change in him. At least, there seemed to be a change, though that may have been because she had built up such an idealised portrait of him. He was older than she had thought, and there was something malignant about him. He crouched rather than sat. His hands twitched nervously. He looked scared, yet indefinably anticipatory. Nora knew that he had certainly not come down to see her, and she was unexpectedly relieved. He was a small, unprepossessing man, with his creased forehead and eyes never at rest. His nose was faintly pockmarked at the end, and although he could not have been much more than forty, he was going raggedly bald, his lank, dark hair smoothed back from his walnut-shell forehead. No, thought Nora with a shudder, not even if it had been a way of escape from the farm: no, not with this stunted little clerk, bringing with him the atmosphere of his Liverpool office. Even if he had come because of her — and now she was quite positive that he had not done so. She wondered again what could have brought him; and, glancing at her mother, she saw that she, too, was puzzled.

'It's a small world,' said Mr. Jonathan, with an important little cough.

He obviously wanted their attention for what he had to say.

'I made some surprising discoveries when I was down here last time,' he went on, turning around to face the room. He looked about, at the clock with its pendulum doggedly nodding from side to side in its glass case, at the calendar advertising cattle cake, and at the hooks in the beams of the ceiling. 'I didn't like to say anything until I'd been back to Liverpool and made sure that it all fitted. It seemed too good to be true, after all these years — centuries, rather. But it's true. No mistake about it. I always like to be sure of my facts: I'm a careful man.' He beamed. 'This' — his voice rose and he waved his hand, with its bitten nails, all-embracingly — 'was the home of my family. Long time ago, of course.'

Nora and her mother stared at him. The fire glowed behind him, flickering redly behind his drab, saturnine figure.

'The people who had it before us,' said Mrs. Morris, vaguely, 'were the Mountjoys. I don't know who there was before them.'

'It was a long time ago,' said Mr. Jonathan. 'Long before this house itself was here. We're an old family, you know — very old. Came from the Continent. It's all in the books you've got in the other room. I was delighted to find them . . . oh, yes, delighted. Our ancestral home — our entrance to Britain. A gateway, as it were.' And he smiled to himself as though hugging some strange secret.

'In the books?' said Nora.

'Our whole history is there.'

'But I didn't think any of them dealt with family history of any sort.'

'The history of what came before history was written,' he murmured, so that she could hardly hear him.

He was trying to sound important, she decided. She had met them before, these little clerks who talked big when they came to the country, as though being a city dweller gave them some superiority over farmers and the like.

Mr. Jonathan got up from his chair. 'I'm dry now,' he said. 'Perhaps I could have another glance at the books, if you don't mind? Checking up, and so on. Mustn't make any mistakes.'

'Welcome,' said Mrs. Morris, who had been listening with only half an ear. 'But it's cold in there. We could light a fire,' she added doubtfully.

'Quite understand,' said Mr. Jonathan. 'Fuel shortage . . . No, I wouldn't dream of it. It's very kind of you to have me at all. I just want to look at a few odds and ends — won't stay long. Too freezing for the fingers, eh?'

His trousers were wrinkled and twisted, stiff where they had dried. When he went towards the door and out into the passage, he moved eagerly, like a traveller nearing his goal.

They watched him go. Mrs. Morris said:

'Still, he's not as funny as that old minister we had for weekends all that summer. Drawing pictures he was in a book out on the lawn, and what pictures they were. Do you remember him, Nora?'

'Yes, mother,' said Nora automatically, her eyes still on the door. 'I remember.'

She heard her father splashing across the yard.

'And to think he's only come to look at those old books!' said her mother with her little explosive hiccough of a laugh. 'They're all the same.'

Mr. Morris was stamping his feet on the thickly-encrusted step. Nora waited, pervaded by a sort of jeering resignation. She knew how the latch would crash as her father put his hand on it, how the coats on the back of the door would mutter as the door opened, and already in her ears, like an echo that has come too soon, even before the sound has been made, she could hear the grinding noise as the woodwork met the uneven tiles. This is serious, she thought. When little things like that get on your nerves . . .

The door opened and jarred to a halt as it met the raised tiles. If only things weren't so much the same, day after day; if only something unusual, unexpected would happen.

'Might as well give up,' said her father with a bland smile.

He did not say what he was proposing to give up. He clumped his routine three paces across the room, pulled his chair forward so that the legs snarled along the floor, and sank down with a gusty sigh.

'That'll be all for now,' he said. 'And if it gets any worse' — he favoured his daughter with a prodigious wink — 'I won't be able to get down to chapel tomorrow. A great pity it will be, but they will not be able to say it's my fault, iss?'

Mrs. Morris came to help him pull off his boots. It took a lot of energy for him to do it, nowadays, and made him very red in the face. There were times when the phenomenon of getting old puzzled him, and he would hold his hand up before his face as though to read in his palm the answer to the questions that were, perhaps, beginning to worry him. Sometimes that hand trembled when he held anything — his razor, for instance: Nora noticed that he did not shave so often as he had done in the past. No-one said a word about it, but often her eyes were drawn to the fine silver stubble that gleamed around his chin and up to his ears. He had been several years older than his wife when he had married her, and it irked him now that she should be able to get about so briskly while he felt his vitality ebbing away. Living on the land for the space of a lifetime, giving it all the strength he had, and now feeling that strength gradually seeping away . . .

Nora went out of the room, snatching up a duster as she went. Her father and mother began to talk together. She was sure they had nothing new to say, but the buzz of their voices followed her along the passage.

She could hear Jonathan's dry cough from the parlour. It was a fidgety, throaty cough. She knew that when she reached the door she was going to turn into the parlour. You didn't do any dusting on a Saturday afternoon, but carrying a duster made things look better. There would always be an excuse to hand when she went in.

It was already becoming dark. As she entered she said: 'Goodness, it's black in here. Don't you need a lamp?'

For a moment her voice did not reach him. His head was bowed over a book that he held open, resting on his two hands. She stopped by the door until he looked up slowly, like a preacher about to deliver a text. His eyes were burning with a far, remote passion, but he spoke flatly, without interest.

'Thank you, no.'

He closed the book and slipped it back on the shelf, allowing his fingers to rest on it for a second when it had been replaced.

'Are these books very valuable, do you think, Mr. Jonathan?' she asked suddenly.

'Valuable?' he said, his voice regaining its normal fussiness. 'My dear young lady — oh, indeed, yes. Very valuable.'

'How much?' she said bluntly.

'I beg your pardon?'

'How much do you think they're worth?'

'Oh, I couldn't say how much. Really, I have no idea.'

'But if you think they're valuable — '

'I have no idea of their value in terms of money.'

He came forward, passing her, and going back towards the kitchen. She could hear the clatter of plates and knew that her mother was getting tea ready. The cold began to tingle at her finger-ends. It was everywhere, waiting for you, sharp, painful, ready to pounce as soon as you left the warmth of the fireside, this bitter cold. She could not stay away from the fire for long. She would have to go back. Soon her brother would come back from the afternoon he had been spending with a friend, and the kitchen would be crowded and noisy. It was a large room, and had once held a larger family than it did now, but noise seemed to ring back from the stone floor and everyone invariably wanted to move about at once. Nora would have liked to stay on in the parlour, just for the sake of being alone, but the discomfort would be too extreme. And the darkness made her uneasy. She had never been affected this way before. Darkness held no terrors as a rule; yet at the moment she became conscious of a sensation of brooding menace. If she had another nightmare tonight, she would have something to say to Simon.

The lamp had been lit when she returned to the kitchen. It glowed richly on the white cloth, the crockery, and the knives and spoons, but the corners of the room were huddled in sullen shadow. Mr. Morris still sat by the fire, his wife's distorted shadow flickering across him as she moved to and fro. Where lamplight and firelight blended, the walls seemed hazy and unsettled, beating in and out with a wavering, unsteady pulse.

Mr. Jonathan hovered indecisively at

the far end of the table, seeing nowhere to sit down that was not in the path of the active, bustling Mrs. Morris.

'Sit down, Mr. Jonathan,' said Mr. Morris gruffly, still looking into the fire. 'Draw you a chair up to the fire.'

'Thank you. I will, thank you.' Mr. Jonathan looked around, as though the selection of a suitable chair would be an important matter. Before he could come to any decision, Mrs. Morris, without halting on her way from cupboard to table, picked up a hard-backed chair with one hand and swept it towards the fire.

Mr. Jonathan stared at it, then went and sat on it. He glanced at his host. Nora, cutting bread, watched him covertly. His mannerisms had slipped away for a moment, and he was just a nervous little clerk paying a weekend visit. She thought he was going to speak to her father, perhaps making some remark about 'the crops,' hoping to win favour — as so many visitors did — but as she watched, a cunning gleam came into his eye, and that unaccountably self-satisfied expression returned to his features.

'Here's Denis,' said her father suddenly.

'Pardon?' said Mr. Jonathan, starting violently.

'Denis — my son.'

'Oh, yes. Yes, I met Denis last time. Yes.'

Nora heard her brother coming across the yard, and heard also that there was someone with him. She stood with her eyes on the door, holding the butter knife in mid-air as though to make a lunge with it. If Denis had met Simon and brought him home to tea . . .

The door opened.

Denis had not brought Simon. He had brought his friend from Pen-y-bryn. They were both caked with snow down one side, and it looked as though they both had grey hair, though actually Denis had aggressively ginger hair, and his friend, shaking his head cheerfully, revealed a thick tangle of curly brown.

And then Nora noticed Mr. Jonathan's face. He was staring at the newcomers with unmistakable anger, gnawing agitatedly at his right thumb nail. For some reason he was furious that someone else

29

should be here. Did he imagine that this weekend had been set aside especially for his visit? Nora felt a quite inexplicable, ridiculous surge of loyalty towards her family, and a mounting dislike of this silly little intruder. She supposed he wanted to prattle on about his connections with the house and his family history, with everyone hanging on his words. And if it was not that, why did he look so black?

Denis said: 'I hope you don't mind, Mum — '

'No, indeed, though I wonder how you ever got over on a day like this. Denis, I don't think your sister knows . . . er — oh, dear me, it's Fred — no, Frank, isn't it?'

'That's right, Mrs. Morris.'

Denis slapped Nora on the shoulder with the odious familiarity that is characteristic of brothers.

'This is our Nora,' he said. 'Nora, this is Frank, another of the old Marine roughnecks.'

'How do you do,' she said, very affably because of Jonathan's scowl.

'I've heard a lot about you,' he said.

Mrs. Morris said: 'We always seem to get a full house at weekends, Mr. Jonathan.'

'So I see,' said Jonathan. 'Yes, so I see.'

3

Mr. Jonathan and Denis were seated side by side on the couch, facing Nora and Frank. Denis was quite at his ease, this being his usual place, but Jonathan, despite the assistance of two cushions, was far too low for comfort, and looked displeased. Frank and Denis were talking across the table about Sicily and Italy. Jonathan glowered at them — whether because he felt that he looked absurd or because he considered the story of his family as being more important, it was impossible to tell. The lamplight scored deep lines in his face.

'Another slice of bread, Mr. Jonathan?' said Nora.

'Ah . . . thank you.'

'Help yourself to the jam. Denis — '

Denis, without pausing in the middle of an anecdote about Naples, reached out with his left hand and skilfully manœuvred the jam-pot around the sugar basin and along to his neighbour.

'Thank you.'

'Do help yourself, Mr. Jonathan,' said Mrs. Morris. 'We're used to helping ourselves, isn't it? You mustn't hang back, or there won't be any left. More tea? That's right.'

'And there he was,' said Denis, 'flat on the deck — absolutely chocker, I can tell you.'

'Like a colour-sergeant I knew at Clacton, before we joined up with your mob,' said Frank.

He spoke more quietly than Denis, but his words were well-chosen, and there was a pungency in his anecdotes that Nora found attractive, though she did not allow herself to show too much appreciation. She knew that Frank was glancing at her from the corner of his eye, and knew that he liked what he saw; she was used to that sort of glance, and did not intend to encourage it. At present she had enough trouble with Simon. Though Simon, she thought wryly, was not what you'd call ardent.

Frank turned to her every now and

then, trying to include her in his audience, and she nodded and smiled politely. He wanted to see her full-face, she knew. As he reached the end of his story — it was much better than the one Denis had told, which, like so many war reminiscences, had meaning only for those who were actually present when the incident occurred — she turned and watched him, frankly appraising him.

He had a fresh, open face with a flattened nose that just escaped ugliness. His hair and eyes were dark brown — thoughtful, warmly appreciative eyes. He returned her gaze as he talked, without embarrassment. There was no trace of the local accent in his voice. When he had finished, Nora said:

'Do you belong in this part of the world?'

'My mother and father came here from Kent the year before the war. My mother was Welsh, but I was born in Kent. Some day I'll go back there.' She noticed that he said, 'I'll go back there,' not merely, 'I think I'll go back there.'

'You like it better than here?'

34

'There's something about it: it's in my blood.'

'Like malaria,' said Denis boisterously. 'He gets regular attacks of it, too — his homesickness, I mean.'

'Places are like that,' said Mr. Jonathan abruptly, breaking in so unexpectedly that even Mr. Morris, stirring his tea in his usual way, the spoon going unceasingly round and round as though he could not halt it, looked up. 'They get hold of you,' said Jonathan. 'Even across generations, you know. Something grips you . . . ancestral memories. I've met some people in my time — I belong to a society that — ah — brings together many such people.' He cleared his throat impressively. 'People who could tell you things that would surprise you. Take the case of my own family now — '

'Mr. Jonathan was telling us,' Mrs. Morris said to her husband from down the table, her lilting Welsh voice coming like a song after the visitor's moist tones, 'that his family owned this farm once — before the Mountjoys, that is. Of course, we didn't know much about all those who came before the Mountjoys.

Funny, isn't it, how things happen? More tea, Mr. Jonathan?'

'Thank you, no. Yes, we belong here. There are, of course, many branches of the original family, who were not all called Jonathan. They had another name in the old days, our family, and they were very important.' He favoured them with a sinister smile. 'Fortunes change; families change; those who were once in power are superseded. But not forever. No, there are some old dynasties that cannot be trampled down for all time. The world needs those on whom it once relied. Rebirth: the world needs rebirth.'

There was an embarrassed silence. 'Here's queer goings-on for you,' said Mrs. Morris silently along the table to her daughter.

'The Mountjoys hadn't been here long,' said Mr. Morris remotely. He supped his tea. 'Nice people. A pity for her when he passed over.'

His irrelevance was welcome. His habit of starting to talk at random had averted many family disputes in the past. He was a man who liked peace in his household.

'Funny ideas about the place, they had. The old woman — '

'She was younger than I am,' said his wife eagerly, 'and you, for that matter.'

'Mrs. Mountjoy,' Mr. Morris went on imperturbably, 'couldn't abide the house. She couldn't understand why the old man had wanted to start farming here at all. Said it was too lonely. She was English.' Perhaps he was being scornful; it was hard to say.

'She told me how glad she was to be going when the old man died,' his wife confirmed. 'Eerie, she said it was — but what would there be about this house, now? It suits us all right.'

She looked proudly around the table. The Morris family had made a success of the farm; even during the war, with Denis away, they had carried on.

'A place like this,' she said in defiance of some unknown critic, 'needs a family, and a family that's not afraid of hard work, mind.'

'Iss,' said Mr. Morris.

Husband and wife did not look at one another, but for a moment the bond between them was almost a tangible thing. Frank glanced at Nora with an understanding, appreciative smile.

'And the books?' said Mr. Jonathan. 'Were the books brought here by the Mountjoys?'

Mr Morris shrugged. 'Couldn't say.'

'I'm sure they weren't,' said Denis. 'Wasn't there some tale about the family that had lived here before? There was the tragic death of the eldest son, or something, and then the parents died, and a lot of stuff was left . . . or something.'

'Most probable,' said Jonathan knowledgeably. 'That is how these things happened. Libraries split up by unforeseen accidents — documents scattered . . . all the threads to be picked up. Years of searching, wandering . . . ' He subsided into a vague muttering.

Mr. Morris pushed back his chair, got up, and went to the door. He opened it and peered out.

'Coming down heavy,' he said without surprise. 'Like to keep on.'

Mr. Jonathan coughed. 'Awkward getting about. Deeper all the time. Perhaps our young friend here — Mr. — er . . . do you think you'll be able to reach your home without difficulty?'

There seemed to be a hint in this that Frank ought to be leaving. They stared at him. Denis twitched his eyebrows aggressively, and a flush dabbed upwards from his cheeks towards his sandy hair. He said, sharply:

'What about you, sir? When are you planning to go back?'

Mr. Jonathan looked blank. 'Back?' he pondered, and then looked amused. 'Back?' he repeated. 'Well, now. Monday morning, I suppose.'

There was an indefinable arrogance in his manner that jarred on those who were accustomed to the generally harmonious, uncomplicated nature of the small talk in this kitchen. He had struck a foreign note that left them uneasy.

'Very bad weather to be out,' said Mr. Jonathan, as though issuing a command to Frank. 'I don't know how you people find your way about this countryside in the dark, especially when it snows like this. Wonderful instinct you must have.'

'We manage all right,' said Denis.

His father, looking down at his plate and wiping a crumb from the corner of his mouth, said: 'It's the men way up in the hills who feel it most. We're not far from the village, and this is a sheltered spot, below the castle, like. But up there, when the wind blows drifts over the roads — and them not being much as roads to start with — then it's hard to get anywhere, and the cold gets at the sheep, and . . . oh, now,' and he wagged his head, 'there's bitter it is up there. We haven't anything we'd complain of.' He drew his chair up to the fire.

Mr. Jonathan was last to leave the table, twisting himself around the corner as though pivoted on his stomach. There was a moment of indecision, when everyone was standing up and chairs were pulled out at awkward, irrelevant angles. Jonathan looked fleetingly at Frank, then sullenly at his shoes. Denis said: 'Well, when we can get the place tidy . . . '

Mrs. Morris pounced suddenly on the table. She and Nora removed the crockery and carried it through into the scullery, where a small lamp burned above the sink. Frank made a move to help, but there was something so brisk and methodical about the way they carried tottering plates and saucers, and finally removed the tablecloth with a practised twitch of the hand, that made him feel clumsy and helpless.

'This won't be much of a weekend for you, Mr. Jonathan,' said Denis, not without a touch of malice.

Jonathan seemed to have recovered his good humour. He smiled enigmatically. 'Oh, I don't know. We'll see what turns up. We'll see.'

They drew chairs up to the fire, the cold weather and the lure of the flames forcing them into an apparently sociable huddle. The sound of running water and the jangle of plates came from the scullery. Outside, the wind was rising, but the atmosphere here was warm and seductively comfortable.

'We could play cards,' said Denis, but no-one made any reply. His father settled down with the morning paper, which had been delivered very late that morning,

41

and at which he had so far only glanced. After a few minutes he was sound asleep, occasionally grunting and twitching his fingers on the rustling pages.

Frank said: 'A fire like this makes you lazy. I ought to be getting up and starting off.'

'But it's early yet. Half-an-hour's walk — '

'That's under good conditions. I mustn't leave it too late.'

Jonathan perked up.

'Don't worry,' said Denis. 'By the way, did I ever tell you . . . were you with us, or weren't you, in Augusta, that time . . . '

Jonathan's petulant expression returned. It was the first thing Nora noticed as she came in, patting her hair into place, and it gave her a swift, unaccountable twinge of unease.

Chairs were scraped back to make room for her. Jonathan said:

'Well — hm, perhaps if I could fetch in one of those books, to check up the . . . ah, the things I came down about . . . '

'I'll get you a light,' said Nora. She took

the torch from behind the tea caddy on the mantelpiece.

'And while I'm up,' he said, rising twistedly to his feet, his shadow leaping tortuously away from the lamp-light, 'perhaps you could show me a window from which I can see the castle.'

'What on earth for?' said Denis.

'A passing whim, if you like. A place of many associations, the castle of Lyomoria — the Tellurian Gate.'

'Never heard it called that before.'

'Nor have I,' said Frank. 'It's been associated with Gwyn ap Nudd, and of course, like every Welsh castle, with King Arthur — '

'Older!' sneered Jonathan. 'Much, much older.'

'I'll show you the passage window,' Nora offered, 'but you won't see anything; it's far too dark.'

As they left the room, she heard Frank saying: 'I really must push along, or I'll be needing a search party sent out after me.'

She held the torch out, conscious of Jonathan moving beside her, his feet catching in slightly uneven tiles in the passage that she avoided automatically. The window, when they reached it, was a dim grey frame for the deep blackness outside — a blackness spotted by clinging white flakes that were tossed by invisible hands towards the smeared glass.

'It's up there,' said Nora, holding out the torch to their guest so that, having satisfied himself that there was nothing to be seen from the window under these conditions, he could proceed on his way to the parlour and select the book he wanted, 'but you can't see any of the castle tonight.'

He took the torch from her and it went out, leaving them in darkness. She felt certain that he had thumbed the switch back, and was reminded of Christmas parties when this sort of thing had happened. But this wasn't Christmas, despite the world outside. He was close to her, and she was for the first time aware of a slight, bitter smell of ammonia that he exuded — rather like a neglected baby. She said:

'The light — '

'We can see the castle now.'

'Surely not.'

Nora glanced towards the window, expecting at the most a dim shape on the crest of the hill.

'You see?' he said gleefully.

She saw. Like a blurred projection on a cinema screen — the spasmodic cinema in the village hall — stained and spotted by shifting snowflakes, was an incredibly coloured sky, throwing up into unnatural relief the hulking shape of the castle. It was utterly beyond comprehension that such a red, unholy light should have sprung so quickly into the heavy sky . . . and yet more unbelievable, she thought, suddenly understanding that this was a world akin to her dream world, only much worse, more unbelievable that the castle should be so large and complete. Complete: that was the monstrous impossibility! Where she should have seen a cluster of jagged stones, she was looking at a massive building that might have been a reconstruction of the castle as it once was.

'No,' she said, as though the denial would drive the vision away. 'No, no — '

There was schoolboyish pride in Jonathan's voice as he said: 'I've shown you something you didn't expect, haven't I?'

She did not answer, not trusting her voice. The place was evil. Not the frightening way it had been shown to her, not even the grimness of those disproportionately massive towers and turrets convinced her of this, but a sense — an inner, compulsive assurance — affirmed that the whole edifice was alive with a foul life. There was something ghastly lurking behind the long, narrow slits in the towers; something perverted and gross that peered over the battlements . . . an invisible but undeniable movement, like a great heaving and jostling that would soon break open the walls like a chicken forcing its way out of its egg . . .

'This is what once existed,' said Jonathan at her ear. 'I knew I could bring it back like that. It proves I'm right. What existed once,' and he nudged her elbow with excitement, 'will exist again.'

Nora took a frightened, desperate step towards the window in the hope that the vision would fade. It did not fade. The lurid red glow continued to dance behind the menacing pile. Hoarsely she said:

'There's a fire somewhere.'

'Fire,' admitted Jonathan, 'of a sort.'

'But the castle? It couldn't be. What . . . how did you — '

'There is an old word for it,' he said. 'The Celts call it *glamourie*. I have shown you a vision. That's only one of my powers.'

The rasping, cocksure little voice was incongruous. It did not accord with that terrifying picture in the window-frame. But the vision was real enough, and somehow or other Jonathan had created it.

Nora wanted to move away. She did not know how long she would have been compelled to stand there had not the kitchen door opened, admitting a flood of light into the passage. The glow in the sky was quenched at once, and all she saw in the glass was the pale reflection of herself and Jonathan, and the inexorable snow-flakes falling slantingly towards them.

Denis came out. 'Come for Frank's

coat,' he said, as though it was necessary to apologise for having intruded on them. He slipped his friend's coat from a hook in the passage wall, and turned away. Nora followed him into the kitchen, and heard her mother give a startled gasp.

'What's the matter, girl?'

'You look as though you'd seen a ghost,' Denis said. 'Was old Jonathan telling you some weird tales out there?'

Nora did not reply as sharply as she would normally have done. It was too much of a pleasure to be back in the kitchen, with the lamp hanging from the ceiling, its circle of light holding back darkness and the powers of evil.

'What is it?' asked Denis with an unusually solicitous note in his voice. 'If that little squirt — '

'It was nothing to do with him,' Nora forced herself to say, unable to attempt any description of the truth. Already, thinking how insane it would sound to anyone else, she was beginning to doubt whether it had not been an hallucination.

Frank, with his coat on, made his farewells, looking at Nora for a long moment as she stood beneath the lamp, her hair like crimson against the unnatural pallor of her face. He said:

'I don't suppose I'll see you all again until the weather has taken a turn for the better. I hope you manage all right.'

'Goodnight,' they said.

He opened the door, and half-closed his eyes.

'Strewth!' said Denis.

The sound of the wind had been fairly subdued, but there was great force behind the snow that struck at Frank's face. It rustled and whispered, confiding to him that he was going to have difficulty in reaching home.

'You'd better not go,' said Denis.

'I've got to go sometime, old man.' He peered forward, trying to discern definite shapes in the shifting, criss-cross patterns. 'There's someone coming.'

'Visitors — at this time?' said Denis, closing the door behind him and standing on the step in order to block the light and see better.

They heard a faint cry

Denis answered it, and the vague figure

that at first had seemed only a figment of their imagination came stumbling towards them.

'I never thought . . . ugh . . . be able to make it.'

Denis took one arm and Frank supported the other. They opened the door and led the newcomer inside. He was breathing painfully, as though he had come a long way, exhausted by the effort of continually forcing his reluctant legs through the piled drifts. His hair was set hard with frosty whiteness, forced over his head like a glittering, tight-fitting cap.

Mrs. Morris got up at once, concern showing in her face. She asked no questions, but took the man's heavy coat and gave him a towel. He slumped into a chair. Mr. Morris stirred, and his paper slipped over the edge of his knee, but he did not awaken.

Jonathan appeared in the passage doorway, a book in his hand. He did not seem annoyed by the arrival of yet another visitor, as one might have expected. In fact Nora, glancing at him, saw that this time he was smiling with deep approval.

4

'A full house we are having,' said Mrs. Morris, without annoyance.

The newcomer had been made comfortable and given a drink of hot rum — 'Not up to the old naval rum ration, eh, Frankie boy?' said Denis — and was now seated in the semi-circle. Mr. Morris had heaved himself painfully up from his slumbers and gone outside to make a tour of the outhouses, but he was not away for long.

'Piling up,' he said briefly on his return. 'Have to dig for the milk to-morrow.'

He slumped back into his chair, fumbled for his pipe, and began to stuff tobacco in with blue, cold fingers.

Frank said: 'I'm terribly sorry I didn't start out sooner. I'll be an awful nuisance — '

'No nuisance at all,' said Mrs. Morris. 'I hope your mother and father aren't worryin' about you. Still, they know

51

you're here. A dreadful night, that is what it is — no night for anyone to be out.'

Automatically they turned to the stranger, whose first breathless, spluttered remarks had not made any coherent impression. Now the cold had been drawn from his limbs and he had had time to collect his wits. He began to explain, reciting the story, thought Nora, as though it had been learnt off by heart, every now and then addressing himself to Jonathan, whose gentle nods seemed to be nods of approval and confirmation.

'I'm sorry I've had to trouble you like this. It's my own fault — I oughtn't to have tried walking over here, but I wanted to see the view from the top of the Horse.' He referred to the mountain known as the Horse of Gwyn ap Nudd, a humped peak that stood arrogantly above the surrounding hills and valleys. It was not a stiff climb, and an ardent hiker might have been pardoned for wanting a glimpse of the great white blanket over the countryside, bulging and wrinkled over Wales, then flattening out and lying smooth and dazzling upon Shropshire.

The only false note was struck by the man himself: he was not in the least like a hiker. 'I thought I could make it easily,' he said. 'I wanted to have a look from the top, just so I could say I'd been, and then I was going to get down on to the main road near Plas Mawr.'

'The main road would not have been easy to find,' said Mr. Morris.

The stranger waved one stubby hand and grinned. He had a tooth missing from the front of his mouth. 'That was just it,' he said. 'I missed it altogether, and got mixed up with a lot of hills. As fast as I got up one, expecting to see a village of some sort, there was a slope downwards and then more hills. I knew the castle when I saw it, and I made for it, 'cos I knew once I was over, I could get down to Llanmadoc. But it was dark by the time I made it, and what with the snow and the darkness, I don't think I could have got down to the village. It was lucky I saw your light.'

'Quite a walk you've had, Mr. — er — '

'Brennan.'

When he had spoken of the darkness, a

sudden fantastic idea had come to Nora. She remembered, all too vividly, the vision that Jonathan had conjured up, and for one wild moment she wondered if he had also called up this man Brennan, a fiend in human shape. All the ghost stories she had ever read, the lurid films she had seen, and the more dubious illustrations in the books that stood in the parlour bookcase, all these came to the aid of her imagination, and she looked at the stranger with an indefinite but compelling dread.

Her fear died away. If this was a demon that Jonathan had summoned, it was an inoffensive demon. Brennan looked like a shopkeeper, with a worried, pimply little face and one ear that stuck out grotesquely, as though — Nora could have laughed now — as though weighed down by the weight of too many pencils resting on it. He would not look directly at anyone except, for brief spaces of time, at Jonathan, but sighed at intervals and fumbled with scraps of paper in the pockets of his jacket. Twice Nora caught those glances that he exchanged with

Jonathan, like a nervous shop assistant who hopes he has not offended an influential customer.

'Perhaps,' he said, 'if you would be good enough to lend me a light of some sort, I could try to reach the village.'

'Not safe,' said Mr. Morris sleepily, opening one eye. 'Drifts there are that you would get caught in. The snow do give under you if you don't know every little turn of the ground. Tomorrow, when you can see where you are going.'

'That's very kind of you.'

'For a lonely place,' said Nora ironically, 'we get a lot of visitors.'

They all laughed, and for a while, in a babble of general, more or less light-hearted conversation, it appeared that the cloud of unrest that had clung to the house all day would be dispelled. But Jonathan and the newcomer, Brennan, were held together by some mysterious bond. Nora wondered whether anyone else sensed this as acutely as she did. There was something between the two men, and she could not believe that this meeting had been an accident. Come to that, she could not believe that any of today's occurrences had been accidents: from the moment she awoke this morning she had been conscious of the existence of a certain fatalistic pattern into which the lives of all present had been woven. Things were moving towards a climax. These strange comings and goings — though so far, she thought, there had been a pronounced lack of goings — all meant something that would soon be revealed. She could not imagine where she had picked up these ideas, but they had in the last hour or so become an obsession. Now she was waiting. Waiting, not knowing what she was to expect.

Jonathan stood up, holding the book that had been lying open on his knee.

'Interesting,' he muttered, apparently referring to something he had read. 'Would you mind if I went out for a stroll around the buildings?'

Brennan tensed. Nora, with her new, unaccountable sensitivity, felt this at once. So this whim of Jonathan's — for such it seemed on the surface — was a part of whatever was being planned.

Her father said drowsily: 'You could have come round the barn with me if you'd wanted a stroll, and done a bit of heaving on bolts, eh?' He snuffled spasmodically, and this time fell sound asleep.

'You'll get wet, out in that,' said Mrs. Morris indignantly. 'Better wait until you can see instead of splashing about this time of night. No sense in it.'

'I'll be safe, I promise,' said Jonathan. 'A little breath of night air — the raw wind of the great wild mountains, as it were.' He giggled excitedly. 'Back in a minute — just steeping myself in the atmosphere, that's all.'

Brennan watched him go.

Denis said scornfully: 'Steeping himself in the atmosphere — that's rich, if you like. Hope he gets well and truly steeped in it: soaked in it.' He picked up the book Jonathan had left on the chair. ' "The Gates of Fomoria",' he quoted. 'Where's Fomoria?'

'Under the sea,' said Frank.

'What do *you* know about it?'

'I read about it once, somewhere, a

long time ago. It's the home of an evil race who came before there were any human beings — all the usual stuff, you know. The Fomorians were old gods who ruled a bleak, horrible world, until the powers of light came to overthrow them. I can't remember the details — I expect there'll be plenty in this book' — he tapped the black, wrinkled cover with one long, brown finger — 'but I believe there was a colossal struggle, spiritual and physical, and the Fomorians were flung out of this world. Under the ocean, or something.' He grinned apologetically. 'I'm not well-up in my folk-lore, I'm afraid.'

'Better than we are,' said Denis. 'It's always the same: when I go to London and meet some pals, I have to show them — Londoners, mark you — where we can go to get a good meal.'

'As if you ever ate anywhere else but a canteen!'

'That's enough, brother. Not any more, anyway. We're free now. And as I was about to say when I was so rudely interrupted, I never yet met a Welshman who knew any of his own fairy stories. I don't myself: I used to like Hans Andersen.' He laughed immoderately, as though he had made a great joke.

'This is not exclusively a Welsh story,' said Brennan in a timid voice. 'It's ancient. The earliest Gaelic name for the gods who overthrew the dark rulers of the earth was Tuatha de Danann. But that's only symbolical, really.'

He was silent again, unhappily withdrawn. Denis wagged his head. 'How come that we get all this sort of talk? Last night Simon, to-day Jonathan — then you, Frank, and now you, Mr. Brennan. You make me feel bloomin' ignorant.'

'It's the weather,' said his mother calmly.

They marvelled at her.

'It's funny,' said Nora, finding that she had become interested in this topic of conversation, 'that so many of those old stories resemble one another.' She was remembering things Simon had said: they had bored her at the time, but now she was quite eager to discuss them. To-night, with the house wrapped in its baffling

59

new cloak of mystery, they were reasonable, credible things — important things. She said: 'All these tales of dark gods and white gods — '

'The goodies and the baddies,' chuckled her brother, 'like in a cowboy film.'

'Like in anything at all,' said Nora. 'The same two sides come up in every story and legend that I've ever heard. I remember we used to hear about them at school. There was one master — Mr. Hemingway, remember, Denis? — who left because they thought he was too advanced for the children. He used to tell us that all religions came from basic ideas and that we ought to study the similarities and think them over before we made up our minds about any one of them. He hated Mr Jones the Chapel.'

She laughed. Frank smiled at the swift glint of her small, even, white teeth.

He said: 'It's a pity they can't let schoolmasters be more interesting. Passing on all the old myths — '

'They're not myths,' said Brennan excitedly, 'they're fact.'

Another of Simon's breed, thought

Nora wearily. What series of coincidences brought them to this house? Coincidence . . . ? A chill of apprehension again. She asked:

'Did you know Mr. Jonathan before you met him here?'

The question took Brennan unawares. He moistened his lips and made a gesture that was ludicrously reminiscent of Mrs. Morris reaching for her apron to wipe her hands nervously and unnecessarily.

'No,' he said. 'No, I never met him before. What makes you ask?'

'I don't know. It just occurred to me. You seem to be interested in the same things.'

'Perhaps you met at some spook society convention?' said Denis facetiously. He, too, was curious.

Brennan shook his head.

'I wonder if Mr. Jonathan is all right, out there?' said Mrs. Morris. 'Out in that snow — silly, he was, to go out like that. Denis — '

'You don't expect me to go out, do you, Mum?' complained her son. 'Give him time. He'll be back: people like that don't get lost in the snow.'

'No,' said Brennan in a low voice.

Jonathan's presence had been depressing; Brennan's was even more so. The dejection in the droop of his shoulders had a damping effect on everyone in the room.

He sat like predestined victim awaiting the hour of sacrifice. Without warning he began to speak: ruminating aloud: 'You think you've got minds of your own, but you haven't. Even across so many centuries, you come when they call. They tell you it's time, and you don't argue about it: you come. If I were to make a stand now and say I wouldn't . . . well, you can never tell what might . . . '

He became aware of his surroundings and stopped abruptly. 'My mind's a bit hazy,' he said apologetically. 'I'm half dreaming.'

'Do you good to go to your bed, now,' said Mrs. Morris briskly. 'Let's see. We must work it out, else there will be a mix-up to-night. Frank, if you and Denis squeeze in together in Denis's room — '

'That'll do me nicely, thank you,' said

Frank, 'and I'm sorry — '

'Go on with you. Now, Mr. Brennan, we'll have to see if you can't be fitted in somehow with Mr. Jonathan, if he doesn't mind.'

Brennan's lower lip quivered. Nora had the idea that he might easily burst into tears. He said:

'I wouldn't want to . . . to be any trouble. Maybe Mr. Jonathan — '

'I don't suppose he will mind. Ask him I will when he comes back.'

'If you'd just let me sleep across a couple of chairs in front of the fire, or on the couch . . . ' Brennan appealed like an anguished dog for their help.

Mrs. Morris, saying: 'There's not very comfortable you would be,' shrugged, smiled, and turned to the cupboard.

The wind dropped.

It was so sudden that they all sat in silence for a moment, wondering what was wrong. There had been no great force behind the wind for the last twenty minutes or so, but it had been sighing and hustling snowflakes about the house for most of the evening, and this cessation came as a surprise, producing a hush as portentous as that caused by a clock that has stopped ticking.

Mr. Morris stirred in his sleep and emitted a disturbed snuffling noise. He did not actually wake up, but some part of his consciousness registered this unexpected change in the weather, and his face twitched unbelievingly.

Denis got up and opened the door, half nervously, not knowing what to prepare for.

'What a queer change!' said Frank.

Denis stood at the door and looked out. The heaped snow was clear and quiet, undisturbed.

'It's going to freeze, by the looks of it,' he said. 'I can see the stars.'

He closed the door again and came back to the fire. He was surprised, but not disturbed. Only Brennan, thought Nora, was disturbed, apart from herself, but it was hard to tell whether his nervousness was due to the surprising calm or to something that had been in his mind right from the time of his arrival here. For herself, she was profoundly uneasy: that hushing of the wind was no natural thing, and despite all attempts to reassure herself with the thought of the presence of her family, she felt that Jonathan had had a wicked hand in it.

But that was absurd. No man could control the wind. What he had shown her from the passage window had been done by hypnotism — by this time she could just about persuade herself of this, though aware that it would not stand up to criticism — but no man could hypnotise the wind. The idea was fantastic.

'I wonder where Mr. Jonathan is?' said Mrs. Morris.

'Stop fidgeting, Mum. He'll come in and tell us that he cast a spell on the wind, so that it would stop,' said Denis.

It was not a particularly brilliant remark. Frank supplied a mild, polite smile, but Nora found the words too close to her own thoughts, and Brennan obviously agreed with her.

Then they heard Jonathan coming. He must have walked softly through the snow until he came close to the path that Denis and his father had tried to keep clear up to the door. Jonathan's feet crunched on the path, and rang the usual two different notes on the flagstone and the doorstep above it. He came in, brushing his coat with great, exultant, sweeping movements of his hands.

'Gone off,' he said happily. 'Here we are at peace again. Quiet, and calm air . . . Delightful!'

He looked at Brennan, his eyes twinkling.

Denis said: 'You didn't get very wet, then?'

'Only at first, and that didn't take long. Soon over. Tranquillity after the blizzard — splendid, is it not?'

Frank pushed his chair back. 'I might have a shot at getting home now,' he said. 'If it's reasonably clear — '

'I suggested you should leave earlier,' said Jonathan quietly. 'You've left it a trifle late.'

He was moving across the room towards the door into the passage. Denis made a movement towards him, then hesitated.

Frank said: 'I think I'll try.'

'I'll come with you,' said Denis.

'Don't be silly, old man: you'd only have to turn round and come back.'

'Well, I'll come part way.'

'No, you won't.'

'No sense in it,' said Mrs. Morris.

'I'll be all right,' said Frank.

Jonathan went out, still smiling. As soon as he had gone, Brennan said, in a choked, urgent voice: 'Take me with you. I want to come with you.'

'But — '

'Much better if you stay the night and be comfy until to-morrow,' said Mrs. Morris.

'No. You go through the village, don't you — that's the way you go from here?'

'As a matter of fact, it is,' said Frank, 'but I really think that if Mrs. Morris doesn't mind — '

'You've got to take me,' said Brennan. 'I've got to try to get there to-night. I *must* come with you.'

5

They stood by the door like two gallant explorers about to plunge out into the Arctic night. Frank said:

'I feel as though I'm making my last farewell.'

Denis wiped an imaginary tear from his eye. 'Our blessing goes with you,' he said brokenly. 'If, despite all the odds, you win through — '

'Hurry!' said Brennan, tugging at Frank's sleeve. His fear took all the cheerfulness out of the situation. 'Let's go at once, before he comes down again.'

'Well, I don't see — '

'Please let's go,' said Brennan, 'before it's too late — before he brings the snow back.'

Denis said to Frank, with an imperceptible nod of the head towards Brennan: 'I'll come as far as the village with you.'

'I'll . . . we'll be all right,' said Frank, knowing that this was an offer of assistance with an apparent madman, but confident of his ability to handle the unhappy little man if occasion arose.

They both took their leave of Mrs. Morris, Brennan apologising for the trouble he had caused, at the same time keeping an anguished gaze on the still, forbidding door into the passage. If the latch moved he would almost certainly faint. Frank struck him cheerfully on the shoulder and said: 'Let's be off.'

There was going to be a hard frost. The snow was still light and powdery beneath their feet, but a little way from the surface it crackled like dry leaves. Above, the sky was glowing, and through rifts in the clouds, which were riding away higher than of late, one or two stars shone coldly. Frank was so certain of being able to get home without difficulty now that he began to whistle softly, and looked about with keen pleasure at the shrouded fences and banks.

'Hush!' said Brennan. 'Let's go faster, and we'll soon be in Llanmadoc.'

What was wrong with the man? Frank remembered a corporal in a landing party who had been suddenly taken like this, reduced to a tense, fidgety wreck of a man merely because there was silence when they had all confidently expected machine-gun fire. But that had been war, when men's nerves did funny things at unaccountable times, and this was merely a cold, agreeable night in a still, peaceful country. He turned to see how far they had come from the farmhouse, and saw the square of the kitchen window and a line of light that must have been the side window looking down the lane. All the other windows were dark smudges in the grey side of the house. And then, inexplicably, he felt that the windows, like eyes behind half-closed eyelids, were watching him. He shook off the sensation, blaming Brennan for it, and said loudly:

'We needn't rush it. Better to take things easy and not dive into any drifts. The land's treacherous at times like these.'

'I must get to the village,' said Brennan, floundering forward.

'We'll get there all right. If you try dashing through this stuff, you'll soon get tired. You sound winded already.'

They came to a slippery stile and climbed gingerly over. The slope fell away more steeply, and a long way below gleamed the lights of Llanmadoc.

'There you are,' said Frank.

Even as he spoke, he was aware of something wrong. The lights of the village were there, but in some way they were blurred and obscured.

'Snow,' said Brennan.

It was snowing between the village and the place where they stood. Instinctively Frank blinked as though facing into a snow-laden wind, and then realised that up here the air was still calm and clear.

'That's odd,' he said with a laugh. 'It's coming down into the valley, but we're free of it up here. That's unusual. It'll probably reach us in a minute or two. Perhaps we ought to put a spurt on, after all. That tall hedge marks the road down to the village. Let's get there and we'll have a track to follow.'

They stumbled across the field to the gaunt hedge, snow clustered on its bare twigs like some gross white blossom.

There was a gap and another stile. Frank put his hand on the top and swung his leg over.

He fell back as though he had come in contact with a brick wall.

'What's the matter?' said Brennan.

'I don't know. Funny . . . Must have been off balance.'

He tried again, more cautiously. The same thing happened — but it was not, as he had thought at first, like jumping into a brick wall: there was nothing hard and resistant, but just something that would not let him pass, something that resisted firmly but without blows, almost as a gale would force a cyclist to a stand-still.

And, he saw as he staggered back, the snow was falling a few inches from his face.

'What's the matter?' said Brennan again.

'I don't understand.'

'What is it? Something's the matter. I knew it would be. I knew we wouldn't get away.'

'Screwy,' said Frank, probing the air with one hand, and finding that no snow was falling upon his outstretched fingers. He might as well have been looking out of a window at a blizzard.

'What is it?' demanded Brennan hysterically, pushing past and trying to get over the stile.

He fell back, sitting down clumsily and gaping at the white flakes that swirled on the other side of the hedge. He said:

'We're cut off. He's done it. I knew we wouldn't get away. And now when he finds out . . . '

He sat where he was, rocking to and fro and moaning.

'Get up, man,' said Frank. 'Pull yourself together. We'll just have to go back to the house for tonight or — no, damn it, I don't see why we should give up. We can try lower down, on the track from the front of the house.'

'It wouldn't be any good.'

'Can't you get up instead of sitting there like that? You'll get pneumonia.'

Brennan continued to moan, saying to himself in a monotonous sing-song voice: 'I didn't understand . . . had no idea. It all sounded so fine, at the meetings.

Didn't know what evil felt like . . . never felt a place soaked in it before. Soaked in it.' The word fascinated him. 'Soaked,' he said. 'Soaked, sodden, saturated in evil, and I didn't know it would be like this. If I hadn't come . . . and now it's too late. Wickedness, wickedness. It seemed all right when we talked — nothing more than a seance, in a way. But not now.'

It made no sense to Frank. He put his arms under Brennan's quivering shoulders and heaved the miserable fellow upright.

'Do you want to get to the village?' he demanded.

'It's no use.'

'Come down this way. It's damned queer, this business — a freak of nature, I suppose — but it can't be like that everywhere. Let's go along the hedge and get on to the path.'

'No use,' lamented Brennan. 'The cunning swine: he's done for us now — '

'Get moving,' said Frank roughly.

They plunged through the snow, raising little clouds like flour in the untroubled air. Soon their legs would be damp and the knees of their trousers would cling miserably, but before then Frank intended to be well on his way home. He kept the hedge on his left and then moved off at an angle that would bring them to the cart-track and the lane. He knew the way fairly well; he had been over here a couple of times with Denis, and he knew the layout of the farm well enough to get his bearings, especially with the lights of the village below. He could not account for the fact that they were, after a few minutes, facing the farm-house, a dark shape with the even darker and less substantial ruins of the castle behind, crowning the hazy slope.

'That's funny.'

Brennan whimpered.

'I'm getting confused,' said Frank. 'I thought I'd got a pretty good idea of the place from my last visit. It doesn't look the same, blotted out like this. Still, if I keep my eye on the cluster of lights up the Rhos road, we can't go wrong.'

Again they struck off, and Frank tried to keep the lights in focus, but found that they dimmed and then sparkled, clouded over and seemed to shift, winking at him sardonically, like distant stars being revealed and then wiped out by spasmodic clouds.

Brennan floundered up to his knees in a swift declivity, and fell forward on his hands.

'Lost,' he said. 'Lost.'

'Of course we're not lost, man. Up you come. We'll make it.'

Frank wiped his brow grimly. He was not deterred. This was uncanny, but he was going on. He had heard tales of the strange things that happened to men on snowy mountains and on the great frozen wastes of the Polar regions. It was a matter of keeping your head. This wasn't the Arctic, and he couldn't go very far wrong. Strange things, maybe, but he was going to stay calm and be ready for them. Snow blindness, mirages, the whole lot — let 'em all come.

But he was nevertheless not prepared for the sight of the farmhouse ahead of them once more. They were at the front, the dark windows gaping toothlessly at them.

'We're going right round the house,'

said Frank. He had no desire to alarm Brennan still further, but he had to speak aloud in order to give himself courage.

'We might as well go back,' said Brennan hopelessly.

'I think it'd be as well. We can leave tomorrow morning. No. No, I'm not going back. One more attempt, first.'

'Not worth it.'

'We can try. Now keep those lights ahead of you, and if you lose sight of them tell me, and we'll stop.'

It sounded all right. It sounded reasonable and intelligent, and you couldn't very well go wrong. But they finished up with the farmhouse lying ahead of them up the slope.

'And I'm positive we didn't turn round,' said Frank.

He understood something of the fear that was clutching at Brennan. His only wish now was to get back inside the house, where there was warmth and company — and sanity. Out here . . .

'All roads lead to Rome,' he said shakily, trying to pass it off as a joke. 'Let's go back.'

Brennan made no reply. He had already begun to walk with an air of resignation towards the house. Frank caught up with him and together they went along the side of the house into the yard. The lighted window welcomed them, and there was a cheerful line of brightness along the bottom of the door. Frank knocked. Nora opened the door. He was conscious of an immediate surge of pleasure at the sight of her slim shape, the light falling on her cheek and the shoulder of her dress. Even now, with an unnatural fear at his back, out there in the twisted night, he thought of the local girls he knew who ran to fat through eating too many potatoes and too much bread and butter, the staple farmhouse diet. He smiled at her shadowed face and said:

'Dare we come in?'

'Come along in,' she said, and he thought he detected relief in her voice. It made recent events look different. 'Couldn't you make it?' she said.

'Failed miserably.' He stepped back into the warm kitchen, Brennan shuffling in behind. 'Here we are again.'

'The bad pennies!' Denis roared a greeting, as though they had not met for weeks. 'Defeated, hey? The gallant trail-blazers turn back, defeated by the elements.'

'That's about the size of it.'

Denis nodded with amusement at Brennan. 'You look worse than you did the first time,' he said candidly. 'Was it very bad?'

'Bewildering,' said Frank.

The two of them were incorporated once more into the group around the fire, which had been on the verge of breaking up as they came in, and he told the story of their futile attempt to get away from the Morris land. Mrs. Morris and Denis looked incredulous. Mr. Morris was awake, but he was browsing over the red coals, and apparently paying no attention. Only Nora listened carefully, her green-flecked eyes narrowed and contemplative; she was obviously weighing his words and not liking what he was saying. What did she know? Once, she made a slight motion in the direction of the passage door, and Brennan also strained towards it.

79

Frank said: 'Where's your visitor — Mr. Jonathan?'

'Upstairs in his room,' said Denis. 'He must be frozen by now. Unless he's gone to bed without saying goodnight. A queer cove. I wonder what he'd make of your story? More Welsh quaintness, I guess. Of course, it's all quite plain: you had a bottle of hooch concealed in your pocket, young Swift. Staggering around like that! Disgusting!'

'Whatever it was that hit us,' said Frank, 'it wasn't drink.'

They heard Jonathan coming downstairs. He came along the passage, and the door opened. The latch fell back with a loud rattle. He said slowly:

'You enjoyed your walk?'

'How did you know we'd been for . . . a walk?' said Frank.

Brennan shrank into his chair.

'Eh?' said Jonathan. 'Oh, I had an idea. A nice night, quite perfect for a stroll. If I hadn't been out once already this evening . . . But no doubt I shall have another opportunity while I'm here.' He smiled benignly at Brennan, then glanced at the clock. 'Surely your clock isn't right?'

Even Mr. Morris laughed. They were fond of their clock, which Mrs. Morris regarded as being a member of the family. It was a large mahogany affair, hanging from the wall beside the window, its pendulum nodding to and fro behind a glass panel. The clock was fast. Sometimes it was an hour fast: this was regarded as normal. Sometimes it varied from this normal by ten or fifteen minutes either way, in which case Mrs. Morris became very worried.

'It's a touchy clock,' she explained to Jonathan. 'Rhys has never liked it — '

'You and your old clock,' her husband confirmed obligingly.

'It won't go for him. Let him touch it, and it stops — right away, mind. If he winds it, stopped it is until I come and give it a shake. And if you try to alter it — '

'Not that you'd dream of altering it, whatever happened!' laughed Denis. 'It's always an hour fast because you like it that way. You like to think the time's not what it looks as though it is when you look at it. That is, I mean — '

'We couldn't alter it,' asserted his mother stoutly. 'No one can touch it at all, except only me. And if you altered it, stop it would, right away. A fine time we did have when you thought you would take it to pieces. Take it to pieces, is it? It doesn't fancy being played with.'

'Old clock,' grunted Mr. Morris.

'It's strange,' said Frank, 'but we always have *our* clock running a bit fast. It's amazing what a pleasant feeling it gives you of being ahead of yourself.'

Nora shook her head and laughed. She said: 'I've never been able to see the point of it. Why not have the right time, so that you know exactly where you are, instead of having to go through a lot of calculations?'

'Logical enough,' Frank said, 'but the matter's a psychological one, I fancy.'

Jonathan leaned his hands possessively on the back of Nora's chair. 'But the right time?' he asked. 'My watch has stopped, and I want to know the right time. If I wake in the middle of the night, you know; like to know the time.'

'Fifty-three minutes fast,' said Mr. Morris curtly and authoritatively.

'Thank you. I think I'll go to bed now. Perhaps Mr. — er — Brennan, you said, I believe — perhaps you'll come up soon, so as not to disturb me? I'm a light sleeper, and if it's all the same to you — '

Mrs. Morris was beginning to wipe her hands vigorously on her apron. 'Oh, Mr. Brennan. Forgetting I was — I hadn't made any arrangement — that is, I can get you some blankets down here if you still want . . . '

He shook his head, apparently past caring.

'I'll sleep in Mr. Jonathan's room.'

'Good,' said Jonathan. 'Good-night, one and all.'

Brennan clasped his hands on his knees, and said: 'I'll be getting along, then.'

Mrs. Morris said: 'Come on to your bed, Rhys, before it's asleep you are.'

Nora stood up. Frank, drowsy, knew that he was staring at her, but in this drowsiness he could believe that no one else noticed, since everyone else seemed

83

so far away. He wanted her to say something. Just the sound of her voice, that was all.

Denis slapped him on the shoulder and startled him into unexpected, resentful alertness.

'Hell's bells, Denis.'

'I wonder if Simon will come over to-morrow,' said Nora. 'He knows so much about these things.'

'What things is it?' demanded Mr. Morris.

'Nothing, really. Just that . . . oh, dear, I'm so tired.'

Brennan said: 'No one can come here to-morrow. Nothing can get in here now, or out of here — nothing human, that is.'

6

'I don't feel sleepy any more,' said Frank.

Denis yawned. 'Don't you? Well, I do. Blow out the candle, will you?'

The candle burned with a steady, straight flame on the chest of drawers that stood by Frank's side of the bed. Frank lay and looked up at the ceiling. A thin crack ran across from one corner to the middle of the room, like a strand of spider's web caught up in the plaster.

He said: 'Would you mind very much if I left the candle on and read for a few minutes?'

'Reading — at this time of night?'

'Not if it's going to cause you a lot of restless tossing and sleeplessness.'

'What — me? I'm easy, Frankie. If you want to strain your eyes, that's your business. What have you got — a dirty book?'

Frank reached up — it was cold when you put your arm out of the bedclothes

— and took down the old volume that lay beside the candle.

'The book Jonathan was so interested in,' he explained. 'He left it downstairs. I thought it might clear up some of these problems.'

Denis yawned again, cavernously. 'What problems?'

'The way we were turned back to the house, for one thing.'

'Seeing things,' said Denis. 'Mmm. No problem there.'

Frank twisted himself round so that the light fell on the yellowed pages of the book. A musty smell rose from the paper. There was no publication date given, but the pompous English made it obvious that the volume was not so very recent.

It was, at first, very disappointing. The tortuous language and non-committal style made it seem like so many vague mystical books; at times, however, there was an alteration, and a collection of dry facts would be stated in a singularly dull fashion. Frank, trying to keep the sheets and blankets up to his chin and to leave no more than his hands poking out to

86

hold the book, wriggled into another position and tried to concentrate. He had a feeling that this hotch-potch of words made sense, if only one could fit the pieces together. There was something elusive about the book: its meaning was evasive, always just that little distance too far to be seen clearly. If only he could stop his mind wandering to the thought of Nora, mingled with impressions of this room, and memories of that incredible attempt to get away from the house, he might extract some meaning. But so far he was not having much success. This section about the priests of an old religion, for instance, was apparently the usual anthropological stuff. The priests were almost certainly Druids: the details given tallied with what he remembered of what he had heard about Druids. It's as vague as that, he thought, and wondered whether he might not be well advised to stop trying to puzzle out matters on which he had insufficient knowledge.

'Found anything?' said Denis sleepily.

'Only the usual business about wielding the powers of illusion, bringing up storms, magic yew wands, mistletoe, and so on. The Silver Bough of communication with the gods . . . hm. This writer doesn't think much of the Silver Bough brigade. In fact' — he turned over a few pages — 'he hasn't much patience with the gods of light at all. It's only the more material things that seem to appeal to him. Powers of transforming one's fellow human beings into all sorts of unpleasant animals. Our ancestors had some nice tricks, when you come to weigh them up. Delightful rites they indulged in so that they would be granted certain powers from those who ruled the air and the underworld. Useful powers, admittedly.' He turned a crackling page. 'Calling on Arawn, King of Annwn, and Pwyll, and Manawyddan and Pryderi . . . There seems to be a mix-up over these gods of the nether regions. They can't all be bosses. Unless, of course, they have different functions, like saints, only the other way round.'

Denis began to breathe heavily, but was woken by a sharp cry and an involuntary movement on Frank's part. 'What's bitten you?'

'This,' said Frank, thrusting the book across to his friend, with one finger indicating a paragraph that had taken his attention.

'Don't be so ruddy stupid,' Denis protested. 'I couldn't open my eyes wide enough to read that sort of print. What is it — the one about the old witch of Endor, or the young lady of Gloucester?'

'The magic powers of the priests. They could cast mists over the countryside, bring on storms, and raise obstacles in the path of their enemies.'

'Nice for them. What about it?'

'Don't you see?'

'No.'

Frank groaned with exasperation. 'The way we were forced to come back this evening,' he said. 'You don't think there's any connection? Jonathan reads a book like this, then disappears for a while. The wind drops, but when we try to get away, we find we're cut off, that the landscape isn't what it seems, and that we can't get past a certain point, whatever we do.'

'Are you suggesting,' said Denis, speaking less thickly, 'that there's black magic going on around here? In the twentieth century — and by that little drip?'

'It seems absurd,' Frank admitted. 'But it ties up so well.'

He felt that the book ought now to be clear to him. He was on the track of something, and it should not be hard now to pick out what was of importance. The candle had a long way to burn yet. The wax was dripping slowly, heavily, down into the dish. The flame continued to stand erect like a sentinel.

But still the meaning was clouded in mystery. What was the vengeance yet to be exacted for the misery brought on the sons of Tuirenn; what was the threatened return of Balor the One-eyed; who were the sleeping ones who would awake when challenged to fight once more, at a Moytura that would be blacker than before? Dormarth, the red-snouted hound, would once more lead the pack . . .

'Come on,' said Denis. 'You've woken me up. Now tell me what you've found.'

'I haven't found anything really definite. I wish these cursed writers wouldn't speak in riddles. 'There shall be that day when the gateway is opened once more, and the Old Ones shall ride back, and the world shall be delivered over again to the masters. Then the names of Arawn and Pryderi, of Black Powys, and Moro with his Black Steed that sets the water ablaze, will be called upon, and beyond, the echoes will answer with the real names of which these are only names.' Clear as mud, isn't it?'

'Sounds nuts to me.'

'There's something about the ring of it that I don't like. There must have been something in the old days to make people fear the Druid priests so much. All these stories of witchcraft and evil wouldn't have come about if there hadn't been some foundation of truth, however small. The sacrifices, the stories that you can still hear in Ireland and Scotland about the evil eye — '

'Now I'll never get any sleep at all,' Denis lamented.

'I'd like to know just how much truth there was in them.'

'It was all fear and superstition. Witch

91

doctors playing on people's nerves, that was all.'

It was easy to think comforting thoughts like that nowadays, thought Frank. What had it been like in the past?

He said: 'What do we really know about the Druids?'

'They wore nightshirts and twigs in their hair.'

'That's the way we see them in pictures — '

'And at the Eisteddfodau.'

'Without many of their original characteristics,' said Frank, grimly. 'We've only heard of them as a priestly caste, whose word was law, but we don't know what went on. History is patchy, and there's a lot of information missing. We know that from the first reliable records available, we can get a full picture of a fully developed religion and social system; but we don't know how it was built. How long had these powerful men been here, ruling the destinies of the people of this island? Were they perhaps only the remnants of an incredibly ancient race that did not exist only here, but all over the face of the earth? There are traces of similar rites all over the world — '

'Where, for example?'

'I don't know,' said Frank. 'This is all stuff I've read. Admittedly I haven't delved very deeply into the subject, but I've come across references here and there, and I know I've always had the impression that the Druids weren't just the crude priests of a barbarous people, as so many folks seem to think.'

Denis sat up suddenly in bed. The wind had started again.

'That wasn't right,' he said.

They listened. There had been absolutely no warning. One moment there had been silence, then there had been the wind. But it was not, as both of them had realised almost immediately, a normal wind. It was a sighing wind, like the sound of a voice calling. It seemed to have sprung up about the farmhouse itself, and Frank felt that it did not blow across the hills. He glanced down at the open book on his pillow. The candle flame had begun to flicker, and the light dabbed at the old, faded print. 'Then shall there be a calling upon Mathonwy and Balor, and upon the names that are the real names.' Same sort of thing again. And the wind called like the sound of a voice moaning around the house. He shut the book with a snap and looked apprehensively towards the billowing curtains across the window.

'Stop looking so worried,' said Denis unsteadily. 'The wind's risen again. It's a queer sort of night. That's all.'

'That's not all.'

'What, then? Is Jonathan behind all this?'

'That's what I'd like to know.'

Denis said: 'If this is a throwback to the Dark Ages, and we're in for a spell of Black Magic, it won't be dished out by little squirts like Jonathan. I don't know what a Druid looked like, but I'll bet he was an imposing sort of bloke, and there's nothing imposing about Jonathan.'

'Physically there isn't.'

'I don't believe there's anything at all about him,' said Denis.

'I wouldn't be too sure. Not that I can visualise Jonathan as one of 'the black family of accursed adepts,' as they are referred to in this little volume of bed-time stories.'

'Nor me. Blow the candle out and we'll snatch some shut-eye.'

Reluctantly, Frank craned up and blew out the candle. He lay back, waiting for the odour of burnt wax to drift over to him. The wind was still making that unearthly noise at the window, and as he listened, unwilling to indulge in the childish but tempting trick of plunging under the bedclothes and muffling his ears, he thought that it became more impatient. It appealed more and more peremptorily. The window vibrated nervously as though a tram were passing the house. Absurd thought. But, he found, a reassuring one: a world in which trams, buses and aeroplanes existed was not a world that had any room for necromancers.

As though to deny this, the wind shrieked once, wildly, and then relapsed into its plaintive, angry whining. Now it was almost forming words. There was a strange blend of rising and falling music and the mutter of voices.

The voices were real.

Frank prodded Denis and said: 'Hey! Wake up!'

'I'm not asleep. What is it?'

'Listen to those voices.'

'That's the wind.'

'No; there's something there, besides the wind.'

They lay staring up into the darkness, trying to hold their breath so that they could distinguish what was real and what was imagined.

Denis said: 'You're right.'

'Voices in the wind . . . ? It seems to come from in and around this house.' They were whispering now.

'Or — or the castle.'

'Good lord, yes. I wonder where the castle fits into this?'

'Search me.'

They were quiet, and in a slight lull in the great sighing of the wind, they heard a foot strike a board outside their bedroom door. A voice said:

'Shut up, you fool, and hurry. Hurry — there is not long to wait.'

Denis said: 'That's Jonathan.'

He slipped out of bed and moved

stealthily towards the door.

'No,' said Brennan's voice.

There was a muttered argument. Frank joined Denis, and they stood shivering, waiting for another sound.

'I won't do it,' said Brennan.

'Don't stand here arguing, damn you. If you wake the house — '

'I'll wake them, all right. I'll — '

'Do you think that would save you now?'

Brennan whimpered.

'That's better,' said Jonathan softly. 'Now come along. If you must argue, argue downstairs, where we won't be heard. But you might as well not argue.'

'They're near the head of the stairs now,' said Denis.

He opened the door slightly, and tried to peer through. Then Jonathan began to speak again with venomous irritation; this time his voice was much clearer.

'What's the matter now? We've been over all this — what's frightening you, you blockhead?'

'It wasn't the same. I won't do it. You're not going to open the gateway.'

Denis giggled. Frank dug him in the ribs

'Sorry,' muttered Denis, 'but all that hissing out there on the landing sounds so silly.'

'I have a feeling it's not so silly. I think it's deadly serious.'

They could see two dark shapes against the lighter blur of the landing window. Jonathan, standing on a higher tread of the stair, hung over Brennan like a vicious hawk. He said:

'The gateway will open to-night. Pull yourself together. This is our hour of greatness.'

'Ours? I know the truth. I should have known it all along. When it's all over, what will be left of me? I'm going to wake them all up, and tell them. As soon as I got here, I knew.'

'You knew? What did you know, puny little fool?'

'I'm a sensitive. You seem to have forgotten that. I know all about places when I'm in them. This is no materialisation you're after. It's something far more than that. This is black evil. This is — '

'I was a fool to choose you,' said Jonathan bitterly, 'but since you're here, you'll go through with it, even if I have to make you.'

Brennan actually found the courage to sneer. 'Not a step do I go of my own free will. And I know as well as you do that force doesn't help. Results may not be . . . satisfactory. There's more danger in it for you, isn't there? That's the way it is.'

'I'll take that chance. I am one of the ancient lineage, and I can afford to take chances. I am a lord of power and of illusion.' He was beginning to speak louder, forgetting the people asleep along the landing. 'Look, little fool, out of the window, and see for yourself the splendour that is to have its birth from your miserable body.'

Brennan looked towards the window.

From where Frank and Denis stood, keeping the door open just enough for them to see the two weird silhouettes that argued and gesticulated at the head of the stairs, it was impossible to see what lay outside the window. Brennan appeared to be looking up at the castle, which lay at an angle from this window, but none of it was visible to the two watchers.

What they did see, however, was the change of colour in the sky. Beyond the window was a dull flickering and then a swift surge of light like the gush of a blast furnace.

It lit up Brennan's pimply little face for a hellish second. He stared, his mouth twisting and his eyes widening. Frank felt sick in the pit of his stomach at the sight of that face. In it was all the inexpressible terror that man could ever have imagined. It was a terror beyond normal moral ken — something that screamed up from the depths of Brennan's being, seeking to show itself in small, ordinary features that were inadequate: this was fear that could not be expressed. Brennan stared, and the light pulsed once more, casting its unholy crimson radiance over his head and shoulders, and illuminating Jonathan, leaning forward, delighted with what he saw. Then the light was gone, and Brennan shouted at the top of his voice. It was a high-pitched, mad, shout, and it went on as he fell and rolled downstairs, bumping to the bottom and then suddenly becoming silent as he struck the tiled floor.

Denis pulled open the door and was out on the landing. Frank paused to pick up the candle and a box of matches, and followed him. Jonathan, who had started to descend the stairs swiftly, cursing to himself, stopped as Frank struck a match and lit the candle. His head showed between the banisters, etched with dark lines of fury.

'The little fool,' he said between his teeth.

Then Nora's door opened, and was followed by the opening of her father and mother's door. They huddled together by the candle, staring down over the rail into the dark well of the ground-floor passage.

Mrs. Morris said: 'Whatever — '

'Brennan,' said Frank. 'He was — '

'Sleepwalking,' said Jonathan loudly. He stared defiantly up at them.

Frank's eyes narrowed. 'Denis and I heard the two of you — '

'He was sleepwalking. A very strange case. He was one of those somnambulists who can answer you quite coherently in their sleep — an unfortunate accident, this.'

'Accident?'

Denis said in Frank's ear: 'Maybe we'd better let him think that we believe him. Keep him here until the police come.'

Jonathan began to ascend the stairs again. 'The poor fellow is dead.'

Mrs. Morris gasped. Nora, moving closer to Frank as though for protection, turned pale.

Jonathan said savagely, half to himself: 'Now he will have to be replaced.'

They did not ask him what he meant. They were tired, bewildered by this thing that had happened in the middle of the night Brennan's crumpled body was carried into the parlour and laid on the couch.

'In the morning,' said Mr. Morris gravely, 'I will go for Williams the Police.'

'If you can get down to the village,' said Jonathan slyly.

They regarded him with hostility.

For the rest of that night Frank and Denis took it in turns to lie awake, listening for any sound from Jonathan, in case he should try to get away. He made no move, however, and Frank was filled with a gnawing suspicion that Jonathan knew all about their vigil and was amused.

7

It was a still, translucent morning. No-one lingered in bed: there was too much to be considered.

Frank awoke with his toes tingling with cold, baffled on the first second of consciousness by his surroundings. Then he realised where he was, and the strange occurrences of the previous night came back, deformed and unreal as a fleeting dream. Surely that hadn't happened? He sat up, noticing that Denis had already left the room, presumably leaving him for an extra rest until breakfast was ready. That incredible incident at the head of the stairs — how had he come to imagine such a thing? It all shifted and changed as he thought about it, but as he swung out of bed and began to get dressed, the chill striking at his fingers as he fumbled with his shirt buttons, he knew more and more certainly that it had all been real. What where they going to do now? How was

Jonathan going to come out of this? There were too many questions to be answered. He must get down and talk to the others.

His eyelids drooped. This was as bad as the night after a watch: sleeping in two-hour spasms was in some ways worse than not sleeping at all. Still, Jonathan hadn't got away — unless, he thought with not nearly as much scepticism as he might have done yesterday, he's turned into a bat and flown out of the window.

He went downstairs, startled by their blankness and innocence. He would not have been surprised to see Brennan still lying at the bottom. One would have expected the aspect of the stairs to have changed subtly, somehow. But there was no blood, no mark.

Denis, looking out of the kitchen, said: 'Oh, good. I was just coming to give you a shout. Come and join us.'

They were seated awkwardly near the fire. The kettle was beginning to sing tentatively. The whole scene was wrong: no-one was at ease, sitting down like this before breakfast. Mr. Morris, a sparkling hint of frost on his eyelashes, stretched out his wet boots and shook his head.

'Best get Mr. Jonathan down now,' he said.

'I think we ought to talk first,' said Denis, 'and keep an ear open in case he tries to get away.'

They stared at a little wreath of steam that was emitted from the spout of the kettle. Its singing grew more jubilant.

'Breakfast, is it?' said Mrs. Morris. 'While we talk.'

The others moved their chairs, and she began to bustle around, but instead of concentrating on what she was doing, she was trying to listen to what they were saying, and throwing in a word here, an interjection there.

'What are we going to say to him when he comes down?' asked Nora.

Denis laughed harshly. 'There's a woman's point of view for you!' he said. 'Not the little matter of murder, or manslaughter, or responsibility in any way whatsoever for Brennan's death; not what we're going to *do* about the man, but what we're going to *say* to him! What do you think we ought to do, Frank?'

'The first thing is pretty obvious. I suppose Brennan really is . . . dead?'

'No question about that. Notify the police, I suppose?'

'Naturally.' Then a thought struck him. 'But suppose we can't get down?'

'Easy this mornin',' said Mr. Morris. 'You can see the way clear. Try you now. Or, no — I will go down myself. I have to go to chapel, and I can tell police on the way.'

'They won't let you go to chapel until they've made enquiries,' said Denis.

Frank repeated: 'Suppose we can't get down?'

Nora, he was sure, understood. She was pursing her lips thoughtfully.

'Remember what happened to me last night,' Frank went on. 'I know you think it was due to mistakes on my part, but I'm pretty certain it wasn't. Unless something has changed overnight, I don't think there'll be any way of reaching Llanmadoc.'

The lid of the kettle jingled excitedly.

'It's quite clear this morning,' said Denis reasonably. 'You can see where you're going, you can't get mixed up about directions, and the darkness won't fool you like it did last night. Anyway, the police have got to be notified as soon as possible.'

'In *my* house,' said his mother plaintively. 'Never have we had police up here, only when there was that party when Joseph the Station broke the dairy window, and he thought that was funny. A thing like this . . . '

'Bear up, mother,' said Denis.

Mrs. Morris shuffled knives out of a handful on to the table.

Nora said: 'It was nothing to do with us. We didn't know anything about it. Mr. Jonathan will have to explain.'

'And after we've said what we've got to say,' Denis remarked, 'Mr. Jonathan will have a lot of explaining to do. Come to think of it, I meant to go and call him.'

'You said we were going to talk first,' his mother reminded him.

'Did I? Oh, hell, what's the use? Jonathan's the man who's responsible for all this, and we might as well have it out with him. Frank and I know what we saw, and there's no reason why we should keep quiet about it. Those two were up to something — what it was, that doesn't concern us — and they had a fight.'

'Not exactly,' said Frank.

'Well, near enough. It was Jonathan's fault. That business at the window, when he showed Brennan something — '

Nora started. 'What was that?'

'A queer light that blazed up — somewhere up by the castle, you'd have thought, though we couldn't see from where we were standing. The way they were talking, you'd have thought Jonathan himself had switched it on. What's the matter?'

Nora told them about her own experiences at the window of the passage, when she had seen the hideous red sky and the vision of the complete castle. 'I couldn't tell you before, because it seemed so crazy, but now it doesn't sound so mad.' There was wonder and doubt in their faces, but not the scorn that might have been there if she had told them at any other time. It all seemed real and close. Denis made a step towards the passage door, then stopped. He said: 'I — '

'I think it would be best for all of us if we decided not to wander around alone,' said Frank. They murmured agreement. 'We don't know what's happening, but it's all very fishy, and if anything weird is going to pop up . . . well, I'd sooner have a bit of company.'

'Good,' said Denis. 'In that case you can come to the foot of the stairs and wait while I go up and call Jonathan. I imagine we're near enough to one another like that. He can't do much with you there, watching me.'

They had now accepted the fact that Jonathan was capable of abnormal deeds, Frank realised. He thought what a waste of time it had been to keep watch last night, fearing that Jonathan might escape. He would not escape: he was here for some purpose, and he would not leave until it had been achieved. Their vigil had been ridiculous. And why bother to call Jonathan down? He would come when he was ready. Nevertheless, Frank said:

'I'll come. We'll straighten things out with him over breakfast.'

It was strange to think of such an important discussion taking place over bacon and eggs. Mrs. Morris found time to lament the fact that no-one would pay any attention to the lovely Sunday treat she was giving them, as she broke the eggs skilfully into the frying pan, but she was all the time glancing swiftly at the door, waiting for Jonathan.

When he came in, dressed in his dark, shoddy suit, he looked serious but untroubled. He gave a brief, affected little bow and took the chair that had been left for him: it was felt that this was too serious an occasion for him to sit on the couch.

'Good morning,' he said soberly. 'A sad day, I fear.'

He showed no sign of reacting towards their manifest hostility. Frank caught Nora's eye. She flashed a smile, and he knew that she had the same sensation of comradeship that he was experiencing: he and Nora were the only two here, he was sure, who fully appreciated the menace of Mr. Jonathan. They did not understand

— they were only groping towards comprehension of this sinister little man — but at least they had no illusions about him. Mr. and Mrs. Morris were bewildered; Denis, stout fellow as he was, could not take in the full danger of the situation: only he and Nora, aware of a mutual bond of sympathy, were attuned to the all-pervading note of fear, a resonance that grew in volume rather than diminished with the daylight.

It was Denis who launched the attack. His clumsiness was an asset: while the others were eating with furious concentration, wondering how to tackle Jonathan, Denis went in like a fearless novice jumping flat into a swimming pool. He said:

'About last night.'

Jonathan studied his bacon reverently. 'A most unfortunate occurrence. I can understand how you must all grieve that such a tragedy should have taken place in this house. If there's anything I can do to help during my short stay here — '

'What yarn are you going to tell the

police?' snapped Denis.

Jonathan laid his knife down. His brow wrinkled.

'I'm afraid — '

'It would help if you didn't act dumb. Frank and I saw you last night. You can rub that silly face off and be honest about it.'

Mrs. Morris said protestingly: 'That will do now, Denis. While Mr. Jonathan is in this house — '

'Let Mr. Jonathan speak for himself. This is no time for being polite, Mum. We want an explanation of what happened here.'

'Doubtless,' said Jonathan, 'there will be an inquest.'

'You can bet your life there will be.'

'Then I suggest that we wait — '

'For our own satisfaction,' said Denis heavily, 'we want to know what you were doing to Brennan last night. I may as well warn you that if you're going to try telling any pretty yarns to the police, we're going to tell the truth.'

'And what is the truth?' asked Jonathan smoothly. 'What were you doing out of bed at that time?'

'We thought we heard burglars.'

'Burglars? They must have been courageous burglars to come out on a night like that.'

'We thought it might be a carefully arranged plan,' said Denis meaningly, 'and anyway, I'm asking the questions. We saw you and heard you. What were you trying to do?'

Jonathan slowly and carefully finished a mouthful before replying. Mr. and Mrs. Morris were silent, apparently unwilling to interrupt their son, but disapproving of this rudeness to a guest. Jonathan said: 'I was endeavouring to persuade Brennan, poor fellow, to come back to bed. Very hard, dealing with sleep-walkers, you know. I fear I have had little experience in the matter. He was a most stubborn case.'

'He was giving you very plain replies. Anyone would have said you were arguing.'

'I believe it's not uncommon. What were we talking about, by the way? It all seems very far away this morning.'

Denis turned in desperation to Frank.

'You can remember the exact words he used, can't you?'

'I think so.'

'Good. It wasn't sleep-walking talk, either. We're both prepared to swear to what we heard. I'm warning you, Mr. Jonathan — '

Abruptly, Jonathan scowled. His face seemed to split up in hideous fissures. There was something repellent about his face, as though he had not washed for months . . . no, thought Frank, something deeper and less ordinary than that. It was a filth that came from inside, and that could not be washed off.

Jonathan said firmly, decisively: 'Brennan was walking in his sleep. I came out to try and fetch him — '

'Fully dressed?'

'I slipped on my coat and trousers as it was so cold,' Jonathan said, daring them to argue about what they had glimpsed in the dim light of the candle. 'I tried to persuade Brennan to turn back. He would not come with me. We argued — talking nonsense, I expect — and then he acted as though he had seen something in a dream, and fell

115

downstairs. A tragedy — a real tragedy — but none of us is to blame.'

Denis said: 'What we heard — '

'We were all very sleepy at the time.'

Mr. Morris got up. 'I'm goin' for the police, whatever,' he said.

Mrs. Morris left the table and went to fetch his coat from the passage. Jonathan made no protest. Denis said: 'I'll come with you, Dad.'

'No, I'll go,' said Frank. 'I must try to get home, and let them know how things stand. I suppose I'll be dragged back for questioning and so on, but at least I'll let the folks know I'm still in the land of the living.'

'We'll all three of us go, then.'

'I think you ought to stay here,' said Frank quietly.

Denis opened his mouth to argue, then nodded. 'Maybe you're right. But don't get lost.'

'I particularly want to go out now,' said Frank, 'in order to check up on myself after last night's wanderings. It's not going to happen this time. We're going to reach Llan.'

The old man had no doubts about it. Slowly he struggled into his coat, brushed his hat with his elbow after his wife had already gone over it thoroughly with a brush, and then nodded to the group of people who were to be left behind.

Outside, the air was crisp and exhilarating. The sun was invisible, but its light filtered through the dove-grey sky and imparted a dazzling radiance to the snow. That great untrodden expanse of glittering whiteness appealed for the imprint of a human foot. You felt, thought Frank, that you simply had to wade in and break up that arrogant surface. A few strides, and the smooth carpet would be rumpled and torn.

Then he saw the footprints that were already there. Away down towards the hedge, two sets of uneven, staggering prints. His own and Brennan's. The wind had blown fresh powder over them, but they were still visible.

'The path for us,' said Mr. Morris, striking away to the right.

Frank would have liked to follow his tracks of the previous evening to see whether they went round in circles. He would have liked to come once more to that stile where he had been forced backwards. But the old man's untroubled confidence made him feel safer: the main thing was to get down to the village, keeping all questions for later. With Mr. Morris, whose calm demeanour had hardly altered, he was in safe hands. Llanmadoc lay below, its chimneys beginning to smoke; the view was uninterrupted by falling snow-flakes or by anything else. The way was clear.

'A bad business,' said Mr. Morris as they crunched downhill.

'I hope the police can untangle it,' said Frank without much conviction.

'Bad for the missus, it is. Worried she'll be.'

'None of you were responsible — nor was I fortunately. It's entirely a matter for Jonathan to fret about, and he doesn't seem to care.'

'Simon was right. Young Simon, he said this man ought not to come, and right he was.'

He offered no explanation, but relapsed

into silence, and they were within twenty yards of the path, its line marked by the top of a small stone wall and a few clusters of bare trees, when they came to a halt.

'What is it, now?' said Mr. Morris.

Frank could not trust himself to answer. That same soft, insistent pressure; the impossibility of moving one more step forward, although the ground was plain before his feet . . .

'Try down this way.' Mr. Morris did not pause to argue or to wonder. He accepted the unpleasant phenomenon and moved away to seek another way down.

The light reflected from the snow seemed to increase in intensity. It was beginning to hurt Frank's eyes. He closed his eyes, stumbling forward, and saw red, as though gazing with closed eyelids at the sun. When he opened them again, the harsh glittering light struck once more, with more cruel insistence. Dimly he was aware of Mr. Morris beside him, muttering to himself.

'No good there . . . we can't get through.'

'Where are we now?' asked Frank wretchedly, swimming in a world of white anger.

'Not far from the house,' was the reply.

He tried to avert his eyes from the ground, and at once the pain eased slightly. Ahead of them was the farmhouse, standing out against its pallid background with a cheerful flaunting of coloured door and window-frames. The edges were blunted by the heaped snow, but the house was clear and real.

Beyond it, the castle ruins hunched blackly on the hill.

'The same thing again,' said Frank.

'Last night — the same, iss?'

'That's why we came back.'

They were silent. The old man, dressed for chapel, looked up in supplication to the heavens. They were grey and featureless. He sighed and turned round to face the village, and almost at once began to blink. The hills, and the valley below, and all the cold expanse of sky, all shone upon the two men like mirrors of brilliant light.

'Let's go back,' said Frank. He was beginning to understand how Brennan had felt.

'The police have got to know. We must get down, else there will be — '

'We can't get through. We'll try again if you like, but it won't be any good. We may as well go back and see what's in store for us.'

The old man hesitated. From far below, the chapel bell began to ring, sending its one shivering note up the hillside directly to him.

'We'll try again.'

Together they walked, stumbled, and pushed, searching for an opening in that baffling invisible curtain. The bell was still ringing, now jeering at them, when at last they desisted and Mr. Morris removed his hat in order to mop his brow.

'No use,' said Frank.

'Perhaps someone will come.'

'If we can't get out, it's highly probable that no-one can get in. Brennan said something to that effect.'

'If they can see us . . . if we could have a fire, or a torch, and get them to come up here — '

'They still wouldn't be able to get in,' said Frank, 'and it would be a long time

121

before any of our friends succeeded in getting the army here to sling a few shells at this — well, this whatever-it-is. Whatever's going to happen is going to happen soon. I have an idea it should have happened last night, and Brennan's death gummed up the works somehow.'

They knew that as they came up the last slope to the farmhouse they would be visible from the windows of the kitchen. The door was open for them, with Nora and Denis waiting, as they reached the step.

'No luck?'

'The wall's still there,' said Frank briefly.

This time there were no jokes, and no disbelief. Nora sat down and folded her hands in her lap. They were all intensely aware of Jonathan's presence. He said:

'Was the going too rough for you?'

Frank did not deign to reply.

'Absolutely no way out at all?' said Denis.

'None that we could find. It seems to be a circle all round the hill: it goes round the other side of the castle, I think, though we didn't try to get out that way.'

'There might be — '

'It doesn't seem likely. We didn't think it was worth while. And the light in our eyes was getting worse. I don't believe we'd have found any way out. It didn't seem much good trying.'

'No,' said Jonathan silkily, 'it doesn't look so good, does it?'

Denis turned on him furiously. 'We've had enough from you. If you don't stop sitting there and smirking, I'll knock your bloody silly face in. In fact, if you don't tell us right here and now what all this is about — '

'Don't come any nearer.' Jonathan's voice cracked like a whip. 'You'd regret it. I will not endure any more of your impertinence. You've seen what occult powers can do: do you want to test them still further?'

Denis hesitated, but his swaying movement and the rapid clenching and unclenching of his fist told Frank that he would not hesitate for long. Whatever the risk — and Denis would probably still not believe that anything could stand up for long against the impact of a large fist in the middle of the face — he was going to hurl himself at Jonathan.

Frank said: 'Stop, Denis. We've got to think this out. Don't do anything silly.'

'Thank you,' said Jonathan. 'Sound advice, Mr. Swift — though I don't know what you intend to 'think out,' as you put it. There is not much you can do in the way of either thought or action.'

Mrs. Morris passed to and fro through the middle of the group. If this should be Judgment Day, Mrs. Morris was not going to let the housework get out of hand, on Sunday of all days.

She said: 'How long will we be up here like this, then? Worse than the winter we did have when Denis was born. What we've got stored away . . . well, it will be a long time before I will make you any more big meals if we are stranded again.'

'How long *are* we going to be stuck like this, without any contact with the outside world, Mr. Jonathan?' asked Frank directly.

Jonathan shrugged, his eyes narrowing with amusement. 'How should I know?

What is it to do with me?'

Denis said: 'Now look here — '

'All right, Denis; take it easy. Mr. Jonathan, there's no need to keep up this elaborate pretence. You've told us enough — or, rather, hinted enough — to make it clear that you're behind all the queer events of last night and this morning. Don't you think we're entitled to an explanation?'

Jonathan got up and walked up and down the room. Mrs. Morris frowned with annoyance. She poked the fire to a blaze, and put her hand inside the oven to test its heat.

Jonathan said: 'Perhaps you're right, my blunt young friend. There is really no need for me to explain, but since it cannot possibly make any difference, I don't see why I shouldn't let you know who is in your midst. You have regarded me as a tripper — a weekend tripper.' He chuckled with delight. 'I played the part well, didn't I? But now I will tell you who I am, and what I am about to do, and then we shall see your faces. I'm looking forward to that. How your faces will change! This is a day in the history of the world and of — '

He broke off, an incredulous expression dawning slowly on his evil face, until this moment suffused with revolting self-satisfaction. He said: 'No. Impossible . . . '

They listened. Someone was coming up to the door of the kitchen. Footsteps in the hard snow, then the ring of the flagstone and the step. The knock.

Nora went to the door, and Frank was sure that she knew who was standing outside. He watched as she pulled open the door and admitted a slim, effeminate-looking young man with sallow features and fine long hands, one of which he put up with a slow, lazy motion to push his hair back over his head — a gentle, smoothing motion. He had deep, thoughtful eyes that seemed sad even when he smiled, as he did now: a smile of greeting.

'Good morning.'

'Good morning, Simon.'

'I've had the nerve to invite myself over for lunch. I hope you don't object. I had a feeling' — he raised his eyebrows questioningly — 'that you needed me.'

Jonathan stood motionless, save for an uncontrollable trembling of his mouth.

8

For Mrs. Morris, life was mainly concerned with food. The preparation of food, the serving of food, and the washing-up afterwards: these activities filled the larger part of her working day. Existence was marked out in sections, and each section was subdivided, different phases of the work being signalled by different sounds: the dull roaring note, slowly ascending the scale, as the kettle was filled; the clang of the oven door; the jingle of knives and forks being scooped out of the drawer; the clink of plates being stacked up for removal to the scullery, and the sound of tap water plunging down on the hard stone sink. At times she would show signs of tiredness, straightening up with one hand pressed against the small of her back, the other tucking a wisp of hair into place, but she did not protest. Nora had never seen her flop down in a chair and profess herself 'dead beat,' nor did she get into a bad temper and accuse her husband, aloud or by implication, of not realising just how much work she had to get through. Mrs. Morris had no complaints. Her routine satisfied her, even when it left her most weary.

Today she did not sit down immediately after dinner, waiting for the kettle to boil up again so that they could have a cup of tea. She did not want to join the nervy, jumpy group at the table. It was better to get on with the jobs that were to be done. She would throw herself into that familiar round in defiance of the growing menace of which even she was becoming dimly aware.

'Nice out now,' she ventured, leaning over to remove the gravy boat from the table. 'Nice for a walk, and you'll be out of my way.'

They grinned at her, but made no move. The tension had been almost unbearable throughout the meal, and it showed no signs of relaxing. Jonathan was manifestly disturbed, chewing his nails and too definitely ignoring the newcomer,

Simon, the only one of the company who seemed more or less at his ease. Nora seemed to derive some slight reassurance from Simon's presence, but he was not the sort of young man who readily inspired confidence: he was too secretive, and when he spoke he was not always perfectly lucid. They had asked him how he managed to reach the house and, with a shrug, he had said: 'I took a bit longer walking than I usually do, but the way was quite plain. I didn't have any difficulty.' That was all he had volunteered, but Nora was sure that the matter would be left there for a short time only. There was more to come. Reluctantly, she left the table and went out to help her mother, who, after one look, said: 'Go back, Nora. I'll finish off myself. Go you and listen to — to whatever's going on. Maybe you'll understand, and that will be a good thing.'

Nora returned to the kitchen. Simon's arrival had inspired in her a momentary feeling of jubilation. If Simon had got through, everything would be all right. She was conscious of a warm rush of affection for him at first, but it had soon abated: ten minutes of Simon's company invariably had the effect of making her irritable, although he was never anything but polite and forbearing. Now, he sat there looking as though he knew what all this was about, but did not propose to tell anyone.

She said, probing: 'You know, we quite thought we were cut off from the world. We were awfully surprised to see you, Simon. How did you get across?'

'I didn't have any difficulty,' he said, as he had said before.

She fought down her exasperation. 'But Frank here, and poor Mr. Brennan, and Daddy, this morning — they couldn't get down because of . . . well, some queer thing that seemed to hold them back.' She did not know how far Frank and her father would wish to be committed on the strange resistance they had encountered.

'The wind, perhaps,' said Simon lightly, 'but mercifully that has dropped.'

Jonathan took out a grubby handkerchief and blew his nose with a great amount of noise. He said:

'I'm given to understand that you, too, have found a great deal of interest in Mr. Morris's splendid collection of rare books?'

'That is so.'

'Are you . . . do you study the subject much — I mean, the matters discussed . . . ?'

Simon rubbed his chin. 'I found the books very interesting.'

'Anything at all . . . special?'

'It depends on what you mean,' said Simon, gently.

Mr. Jonathan did not pursue the matter, but studied the young man apprehensively. His nervousness was some consolation to Nora, who felt that perhaps the danger — that danger that had so far remained undefined — had passed. She looked across at Frank, and saw that he did not share her optimism. He was frowning. He said:

'I think Mrs. Morris's idea of going out for a while isn't at all bad. It would clear our heads.'

'And shake our lunch down,' said Simon. 'But then it's such a shame to shake Sunday lunch down in that rough way. I prefer the languid sort of afternoon.'

Nora came to a decision. 'I think you're right, Frank.' She was pleased — and surprised at her own pleasure — to see that this annoyed Simon. 'I'll come out for a little while,' she said. 'We can't go far, but it'll put everything in a new light, perhaps.'

She was resentful towards Simon, who ought to have cleared everything up on his arrival: she was positive that he could have settled their fears and suspicions at once, but for some reason he had refused. He knew what Jonathan was doing, but he would not put the minds of the others at rest. If he thought he was making an impression as a strong, silent, knowledge-able man . . .

She said: 'I'll just get a scarf and my coat.'

Simon was too fond of playing the part of the mysterious young man. At first she had been attracted by his air of aloofness, but that sort of thing very soon palled. Now, for instance, he could have been so reassuring and helpful — instead of which, he was being silly. She put on her bottle-green coat with the deep pockets, into which she could thrust her hands, and joined Frank by the kitchen door.

'We won't be long,' she said.

Frank opened the door, and they went out.

The sensation of freedom was delightful. Was this all that had been needed, right from the start? Could she have shaken off all that dismal apprehension merely by opening the door and stepping outside into the invigorating air? Probably not: Frank and her father had not fared so well.

She said: 'How do you think Simon got over here? Do you think that — that whatever stopped you has gone now, and that we're all right?'

'I don't know. That's been puzzling me ever since he arrived. He's hiding something.'

'Simon always gives you the impression that he's hiding something: he's worked it up to such a fine art that I wouldn't swear that he was always sincere. There may be nothing behind that appearance.'

'He's got Jonathan frightened, anyway.'

Nora conceded this point. It was one of the few satisfactory aspects of the situation at present.

'But how did he get to the house?' she persisted. 'There must be a gap somewhere — unless, as I said, the whole thing is over and done with.'

'There's one way to find out.'

Her heart quickened as she followed Frank down the slope. It was bad enough sitting indoors and hearing the story of those who had come back after attempting to reach the village: going down the apparently clear hillside towards an invisible obstruction to encounter it yourself was a very different matter, and far worse. She admitted her nervousness, and let Frank lead the way. He was beginning to progress more slowly, with one hand outstretched.

He stopped.

'Still there?' she said.

'Come and try it for yourself.'

Tentatively, she dabbed with her hand, thinking how ridiculous it was to be waving it about in mid-air like this. But it was not so ridiculous when she felt its movement arrested by that unseen wall, force, or whatever it might be, of which she had already heard Frank speak.

'Still there,' he said.

'In that case — '

He said: 'Which way does your friend Simon have to come in order to reach the house?'

'Round the other side of the hill. He can come up and round or right over the top: there's not much to choose in actual time, but coming over the top by the castle involves a steeper climb.'

'Does he usually come that way?'

'I think so.'

Frank turned to face the ruins. Not very far away, but there would be a lot of floundering through the snow before he reached them, and then there was the descent of the other side. He said:

'You'd better go back in, Nora. I'm going to go over and see if there's any gap in this — this curtain, on the other side.'

'I'll come with you.'

'I don't know how deep — '

'You said that we ought to hunt in

pairs,' she reminded him. 'I don't fancy going back into the house just yet, anyway. I'd sooner come with you.'

She could tell that he was reluctant to agree to this. He scented some risk, although the bright snowy slope and the huddled ruins were innocent enough, to all appearances.

At last he grinned and began to trudge upwards.

'Excelsior!'

They passed the farmhouse, giving it a wide berth in case anyone should come out and call to them. The going was heavy, but the effort made them both warm, and Nora had to loosen her scarf. It was a magnificent day. Sun gilded the peaks of the distant mountains and fell indiscriminately on scattered slopes and barely distinguishable farm buildings on neighbouring hillsides. The unfolding panorama of sparkling white splendour was in itself an incentive, urging them to the top, so that the whole world might be displayed at their feet.

But as the castle ruins came closer, the farmhouse seemed to fall away too rapidly: the distance did not seem to correspond at all with the distance they had actually covered. It was doubtless an optical illusion caused by the snow, but it was alarming, and Nora automatically kept closer to Frank, who grinned encouragingly and said: 'Soon be there.'

The castle, so impressive from below, assumed a totally new aspect as they reached the last steep rise which led on to the broken stones and rubble, now dusted with silvery powder: it brooded with an unsuspected malevolence, resenting their intrusion and musing to itself. The holes in the walls became gaping, ravenous mouths. The cardboard silhouette became a three-dimensional, massive erection of crumbling, harsh stone.

They walked under the old arch and stood on the edge of a sudden declivity, beyond which lay the remains of the main wall itself.

'A moat?' said Frank. 'At this height?'

'I don't think it could have been: just a sort of trench to make things more awkward for the enemy.'

'Awkward is the word,' Frank agreed.

'It seems to breathe intolerance and defiance, this place. Bloodshed and villainy, and all that sort of thing.'

'I've never noticed it before,' said Nora. 'We used to come up here and play a lot, and in summer I've often brought a book and read it, propped against a heap of stones. It's never been anything very special. But today the place isn't the same at all. It's come to life — a rather nasty sort of life.'

'Maybe we ought to skirt the castle and go down the other side out of harm's way. No sense in — '

'Nonsense!' said Nora stoutly. 'I'm not going to be put off by queer sensations. I've been having nothing else but premonitions and weird notions all weekend, and I've had enough of them.'

She marched resolutely forward, taking the narrow path, banked up from the trench below, that led to another shattered gateway. It leered at her, and, absurdly, she wondered what lay beyond.

'Something's troubling you,' said Frank. 'Don't go on: it's not worth it.

'Dreams,' she said. 'My horrible dreams

. . . I've got to get over the effects of that nightmare I had about this place. Come on.'

She went through, and even as she passed under the last frail remnant of archway she knew that the castle had changed. She did not see the usual heap of jutting ruins on the other side; she was not at all sure of what she did actually see, but she knew, as she led Frank out on to another patch of level ground, where in summer the trippers carved their initials in the springy turf, that this was not as it should be. They had walked out of the brightness of the snow into a shadow.

She looked up, suddenly seeing clearly, and the world ahead was black.

'Good God,' said Frank, coming to a halt.

There was hard, well-trodden ground beneath their feet. A low wall in a perfect state of repair was before them, and beyond it was . . .

Could this still be Wales? They had never seen mountains like these before. These were raw, ragged shapes, curiously unfinished, as though flung up but a short space of time previously by some gigantic natural upheaval; there were no trees as yet on their naked slopes, and in the shadowed valleys was no life. No life as we know it, that is: *something* moved and had its being down there. It could not be seen, but they were acutely aware of its presence, its manifestation coming up to them much as a putrid smell might arise from the depths of some hideous pit. The sky was dull crimson, stained by the afterglow of a colossal, unnatural sunset, and the ripped edges of the mountains stood up stark and ferocious against its dying fury.

'How did we get here?' demanded Frank in a whisper.

His voice was the pitiful squeak of a tiny animal in a massive world. They had walked into something that had only the most tenuous ties of kinship with the world they had just left.

Nora said: 'A dream . . . '

'For both of us? No.'

And then he dared to do what she had realised would be necessary, but which she had been unable to contemplate. He turned sharply around and she heard him gasp. She put out her hand to clutch his. 'What is it?'

'You'd better have a look,' he said in a choked voice.

She forced herself to follow his example, praying that despite his incredulous gasp she would find the view as it should be — the ruins, and the white landscape beyond.

Instead, she saw the colossal bulk of the castle as Jonathan had shown it to her from the window. From here, caught on its very perimeter, she found it more terrifying than ever. Its very magnitude was something beyond the bounds of reason: nowhere in Wales, a country of frowning castles and citadels, was there such a pile. It heaved its great bulk up against the sky, in itself as fierce and incredible as the mountains that stalked about it. There was far more of it than the hill as Nora had known it could possibly have accommodated. It blotted out everything she expected to see. This was a fortress built even before the one with whose ruins she was familiar, in another land, on a hill that was not as she had known it, in a world that . . .

'What world is this?' she asked.

'Not ours,' said Frank. 'At least, not ours of today. It might be . . . no, how in heaven's name can we tell what, where or when it is?'

'Can we get back?'

'We've walked through something to get here,' said Frank. 'If we walked through, we can walk back.'

He was trying to sound confident, and she admired him for his gallant attempt to cheer her up. In the face of those ponderous walls she found it hard to respond. Then Frank said:

'That gate — right ahead of us.'

He was indicating a low arch, in shape not unlike the ruined one through which they had come. It was impossible to see where the arch led: there was a sort of swirling darkness beyond it, that might have been a mist rising from within the castle. Certainly there was no apparent break in the walls, and it seemed unlikely that a perfectly normal stretch of countryside should lie on the other side.

Unless the castle itself was merely an illusion.

'I've just thought of something Jonathan told me,' she said in a low voice, feeling that it was unwise to speak out too loudly. 'He conjured up that vision for me through the passage window and called it — what was it, now? Glamourie, I think he said. If that was just a mirage, or something he produced by hypnotism, or however you do these things, why shouldn't this be the same?'

'It looks solid enough to me.'

'If we walked towards it, do you think it would vanish?'

Frank looked hopelessly around at the ugly mountains. 'There's no other way out,' he said. 'We might as well take a running jump at the walls and hope to go through.' He strode resolutely across the few yards of blackened ground and touched the nearest wall. It was disagreeably solid.

'This is no illusion,' said Frank.

Nora began to feel the groping of panic at her heart and in her throat. Until Frank had reached out and tested the undeniable reality of that wall, she could not really accept this as anything but a nightmare. Now, following him, she too felt the cold stone under her hand, and knew all this madness was real.

'We could try walking round the castle,' said Frank. 'We're near the end here, and we could at least get a view of what it looks like where — where the farmhouse ought to be.'

'How long have we got, do you think?'

'How long — ?'

'There must be someone here. Sooner or later they'll find us, and then . . . '

'We don't know that anyone — or anything — lives here now. It looks deserted. Come on, let's go and see what there is to see. Remember this spot, so that we can get back and try that little arch if we have to make a break for it.'

Carefully, treading with caution on the unyielding ground as though it might give way at any moment, they went along the side of the silent building that rose above them, approaching the corner around which they would see what lay beyond. Anything was possible. In this world where logic had ceased to be effective, there was no reason why the snowy hills of Wales should not be there: that was their only hope. Just as they were reaching the end of the wall, with no hint of anything but grim darkness awaiting them, there was a sound in the air, far away.

'What was that?'

They paused. The noise was repeated, coming closer, and it was possible to establish the direction: it came from the part of the world that they had hoped to see as home, and this was no noise that would ever have been heard around their home. It was a long, despairing cry — the cry of some terror-stricken hunted creature. The derisive mountains flung back the cry, so that it was magnified a hundredfold, dinning in the ears of the two listeners with fierce insistence. And behind it, muffled but plain, was a confused roaring and howling.

Frank put his arm around Nora's shoulders and drew her against the wall. It offered no protection, but there was a comfort in the pressure of the stone against their backs.

Suddenly a dark shape fled across the sky above them, towards the distant peaks. Behind it — close behind — was a dark, heaving pack of distorted shapes, and from this pursuing cloud came a great clamour like the baying of blood-thirsty dogs. The shapes were shadowy and undefined: Nora, afraid to watch but equally afraid to close her eyes, was glad that the light was not more revealing — she felt that those beings who streamed across the sky were not fit for human eyes to look upon. The pursuers were gaining, she could see. Frank's grasp tightened. Down the sky went the grotesque, screaming creature in the lead, and then, as it seemed to plunge towards the mountains, it was surrounded and caught up by the pack that had been giving chase. There was a second of dark turmoil, then a great, ululating cry that seemed to fall as the heaving cloud itself fell, towards the hidden valley, echoing round and round in a last, utterly damned despair.

Nora began to cry with hard, dry sobs,

shaking with the effort not to scream, fighting down the desire to scream out so that she could hear the echoes come howling back.

There was silence once more.

Frank said: 'God, what have we stumbled into? If this isn't hell . . . '

'Listen,' said Nora. 'They're coming back.'

A rustling and flapping sound rose from the valley.

With it, they became aware of a dim, secret rumbling within the castle; a stirring and activity like a heart beginning to beat.

'They're coming here — I'm sure they are!'

They were so conspicuous that it was only a matter of time before they were seen.

'Round the corner, quickly,' said Frank.

They reached the end of the wall, and looked along the side of the castle . . . to see yet more gargantuan peaks and the shadows of more secretive valleys. There was no way out for them down there.

'Back to the gate: we'll have to chance it.'

'We're too late.'

They shrank down, trying to flatten themselves against the unfriendly earth as the incredible shapes came rolling, stumbling, striding and muttering up the path from below. Some might have been human silhouettes — and yet, as they stalked along to some entrance that Frank and Nora had not noticed before, there was something evil in their movement that proclaimed their complete inhumanity. Travesties of men, of animals, of creatures for which there was no name on this earth; spawn of a reckless, proliferous Nature lost in an insane, lustful fecundity.

Frank murmured: 'They're going. They haven't seen us.'

The last of the party hopped like a misshapen toad over the ridge and along to the entrance. It was gone.

'What are they? Are those . . . those things the people who built this place?'

'They don't look intelligent enough: there's something twisted and sub-human about them that doesn't fit in with a building like this. No, there must be someone higher — someone for whom those awful twisted things are only servants or beasts of burden.'

'Or hunting dogs,' said Nora with a shudder.

Frank nodded grimly, his lips set. 'That's pretty close to the mark, I should imagine.'

They were still afraid to move. The short stretch of ground between the arch and where they lay was deserted, but the silence of the castle now seemed far more threatening than before. There was no telling what might not spring out at any moment.

'We'll have to make a dash for it,' said Frank. 'I can't see anything through that arch, and it might quite easily lead us right into the castle itself. Once we got in, I doubt whether we'd get out. But there aren't any alternatives. We either try the arch, or we stay here.'

'Let's try to get through. That's the way we came — '

'It might be a one-way street,' said Frank with a mirthless laugh, 'but we've got to have a shot at it. There's no-one about now.'

'Isn't there? I keep feeling that there is: a sort of feeling that someone, or something, is slowly becoming aware of our presence here. Something in the castle is waking up, and it knows we're here. Can't you feel it?'

She could not find words to express this indefinable sensation, but there was no need to do so. Frank understood. He lay still, his nerves on edge, alert to whatever message might be conveyed to them, and then he said:

'You're right. And when it's fully awake . . . Come on, we've no time to lose.'

They rose to their feet, completely defenceless, and as they took a step forward a figure appeared in the archway for which they were heading. It stepped from the swirling mists that bubbled within, and Nora caught despairingly at Frank's arm.

Nora said: 'Simon! It's Simon!'

He was beckoning to them urgently. Their minds were flooded with the knowledge that now the entity that slumbered within the castle was fully aware of them, and they began to run towards the arch.

Before they reached it, they saw a burst of activity further along the castle wall. A door had opened, and something was surging out to meet them.

'Don't stop!' cried Frank.

The distance seemed interminable. This was not a dream, but they lived in the conditions of dreams, in which it took interminable ages to run a few yards, while danger mounted swiftly about them. In the brief span of time that it must have taken to cover the short distance to the arch where Simon waited for them, they saw the dim outline of the strange thing that oozed through the door. It was nothing tangible, nothing that moved or walked or behaved in any way reasonable: it was an impalpable, fierce essence of evil, able to strike more swiftly than a snake because it had no substance, yet held back by the sickly weight of its own foulness. Nora's knees weakened.

'Don't waste time!' Simon called, and his voice came from a great distance.

She would never reach him. Her

strength was failing. She was running but not moving. If she were really getting anywhere, she would have covered those few yards long ago. But it was no use now . . . no use at all. This great surging cloud of evil, which was capable of pervading the whole atmosphere, of rolling down and filling the entire valley up to the brim, like tea poured into a cup, would possess her and hold her back; already it was twined about her, gently drawing her back as she tried to run forward to that remote, useless gateway where Simon stood shouting to her. His face began to fade. No use now . . .

Then Frank's arm was about her, and she was lifted bodily through the arch, Simon catching her at the other side and bringing her to a standstill, looking down the gleaming white slope to the farmhouse below, a wreath of smoke curling languidly from its chimney.

9

'You fools!' said Simon. 'Fools — what possessed you to go through the gateway?'

They were going slowly down the hill. Nora felt too exhausted and too faint to walk quickly through the welcome snow. More, she wanted to look around and feast her eyes on the calm white landscape, looking so much more attractive than she would ever have believed possible.

Frank said: 'We didn't go through any gateway. We just walked under an arch, and there we were.'

'I've been under it hundreds of times,' said Nora, 'but I never came out in that sort of place before.'

'The gateway is open,' said Simon. 'You're lucky to have come out again.'

'What gateway is this you're talking about?'

Simon, supporting Nora's left arm, glanced across at Frank.

'There are many things you don't know,' he said. 'I think it will be necessary to clear them up after tea.'

'Tea?' said Nora with a feeble smile. 'I'm so glad we're not late for tea.'

'That would have been dreadful,' agreed Frank, trying to dismiss the thought of what was behind them.

They reached the farmhouse, never so welcoming before. On the step, Frank paused and turned to Simon. 'Since you know so much about all this craziness, perhaps you can tell me what risk there is of that gateway being used again.'

'You mean — ?'

'I mean that if *we* could come through it, there's nothing to stop those — those abominable creatures from following us through.'

Nora paled.

'They won't come through,' said Simon calmly.

'How can you be so sure?'

'They won't come through; not without certain conditions.'

'What are those conditions?'

Simon opened the door. 'That's one of

the things that you'll probably discover later. Not on an empty stomach, though.'

Nora found it hard to adjust herself to the untroubled nods of welcome: she had expected something more rapturous, and found it hard to conceive that the rest of the family should have sat in the house without any inkling of what was going on at the top of the hill. But was it really the top of the hill? More likely another world, another dimension . . . Swiftly she glanced around the room to gain confidence from the clock, the well-worn chairs, the faded wallpaper and the picture on the calendar. This was what she had to cling to. Perhaps if her mind wandered, the ground would slip away beneath her feet, the kitchen would dissolve about her, and she would be back in the territories of nightmare.

'What's the matter, Nora?' said Denis anxiously. 'Have you seen something queer again? What is it?'

Frank came to her rescue. 'Something very unpleasant,' he said. 'We'd sooner not talk about it now — we've both had a bit of a shaking.'

'All right, old son. We'll get round to it later — among other things.' This was directed at Jonathan, who sat sullenly nursing his knees like a wizened old man by a brazier. 'We're going to let our hair down after tea.'

There was no great amount of chatter over tea. Nora felt no appetite. The plate of bread and butter looked revolting. She drank a cup of hot tea thankfully, and waited impatiently for the others to finish. If there were going to be any revelations, let them come soon.

If the experiences of this afternoon had not been so real, she could have believed that what was coming after tea would be merely a game. The familiar appearance of the room and the crockery on the table, the warmth of the fire on her back, and the very ordinariness of everything . . . all these cancelled out the possibility of anything uncanny in the world. Yet she knew it was no good relying on appearances. The world was not solid, but treacherous; not steady, but shifting. One false step, and you were plunged into outrageous abnormality. The ogres and grim castles of fairy tales waited for you through a familiar archway, on a hill where you had played since you were young. There was no certainty; nothing was reliable. She concentrated desperately on the tablecloth, focusing her attention on a small brown stain near the bottom of the sugar basin.

'Got your speech ready, Mr. Jonathan?' said Denis brusquely.

Jonathan's hand wobbled, and he dripped tea over a piece of cake. 'I'll tell you anything you want to know,' he said.

Simon reached out for the sugar. Nora kept looking at the stain on the cloth. Simon said gently:

'Is your knowledge so wide, Mr. Jonathan?'

'Wide enough.'

'How did I get here to-day, Mr. Jonathan — can you tell me that?'

Jonathan moistened his lips. Nora was conscious of a great wave of relief. This might be an anticlimax, but it was a welcome one. Simon knew what was going on, and Jonathan was not going to get away with it. It was a reassuring feeling: it helped her to struggle against the gnawing memory of what she and Frank had so recently seen. Simon could, somehow, deny existence to those frightful impossibilities.

Simon said: 'Wouldn't it be better if you went home, Mr. Jonathan?'

'You're scared of me,' said Jonathan unconvincingly. 'You want to get rid of me. You know what's coming, eh?'

'And I know that this is the wrong time. This is not the right time for taking such a terrible risk, that may result in a catastrophe you, with your puny, evil-grubbing little mind cannot begin to comprehend. You are not the right person for this. According to your books — '

'My books!' snapped Jonathan. 'Yes . . . my books. They're mine, all brought together at last, and they say that this is as good a time as any.'

'Are you one of the adepts?'

'Yes.'

Simon shook his head gravely. 'I think you are running a tremendous risk. For your own sake, as much as for anyone else's, stop before you have gone too far.

Don't dabble with powers beyond your control.'

'It would be pleasant for you if I stopped, no doubt. Who are you: why do you want me to stop?' Jonathan seemed to be regaining his courage, and as he did so, Nora felt her own confidence slowly ebbing away. 'Who are you?' demanded Jonathan again. 'Are you one of the White Adepts — the emasculated fools who are, as usual, too late?'

'They have not always been too late,' said Simon quietly. 'They have kept you and your kind from the books for a long time — across an infinity of generations that makes all this present civilisation but a moment of eternity. Don't underestimate them, Mr. Jonathan.'

'Too late!' crowed Jonathan. 'I have all the books, and I know what it was intended that I should know.'

Simon shrugged. 'So be it. But the . . . shall we call it the assistant? — what about your assistant, now your trained man has so inconsiderately passed away?'

'It will have to be someone else.'

'How unfortunate. It is not safe, you

know, Mr. Jonathan. You need one who has been chosen and well schooled. This is not a game for the uninitiated. Dangerous, Mr. Jonathan, dangerous . . . '

Denis said: 'What the hell are you two yapping about?'

Mrs. Morris said: 'Denis — '

'I'm tired of this,' said her son rebelliously. 'Let's have it out.'

'After I've cleared the table — '

'Leave the table alone.'

'Personally,' said Simon mildly, 'I can discuss nothing with plates and crumbs and dirty cups staring me in the face. Let's form a cosy little semi-circle about the fire. We may as well be comfortable while we hear what our visitor from the great city has to say. A semi-circle, mark you — not a circle. A circle is too potent, isn't it, my friend?'

Jonathan got up from the table, his mouth working. 'You young whippersnapper — '

'Let's finish all this shouting and arguing,' said Denis. Frank signified his approval. 'We'll sit round the fire all right — and let's have some sense out of you,'

Denis added warningly. 'What's going on here? And let's have it in words that mean something.'

Once more they were grouped near the fire. This movement to and from the chairs, taking them to and from the fireside was becoming as regular as a movement in a dance. In weather like this it was only natural — but today Nora felt an undeniable strain. Normally they would sit down as a matter of course, where they could benefit from the warmth: that was all there was to it, and you thought no more of it. But today and yesterday all the moves had been made stiffly and self-consciously, as though they were moves requiring careful thought. Grave committee members assembling to discuss matters of great import . . . or pawns being shifted into position by an unseen hand?

The fire shone in their faces. Mrs. Morris turned the wick of the lamp up, and sat down.

'There'll be no peace till this is settled,' she said wearily. 'Washin' up can wait.'

Nora was more scared than she had

ever been before. There was the most incontestable proof of the abnormality of this weekend! Only a conviction of imminent catastrophe could have caused her mother to leave the washing-up until later. Was she, then, also possessed by this conviction, fearful that they had not a great deal of time left — that the shadow was already beginning to fall on them, its grey fingers groping for the heart?

'Right,' said Denis. 'Shoot.'

'What about your father?' said Mrs. Morris. 'It's here he should be. Wait a minute for him.'

They had noticed his absence. He had slipped out to make a plodding tour of the outhouses. In five minutes he returned, looking incuriously over the little group.

'Come on, Dad,' said Denis impatiently. 'We want to get started.

'What's this, now: a meetin', is it?'

'Mr. Jonathan is going to tell us what brought him down here for the weekend.'

'None of your business,' said his father severely.

'But it *is* our business. What do you

163

imagine all this secrecy has been about, this weekend? What caused Brennan's death, and why couldn't you get down to Llan this morning?'

Mr. Morris joined them and brushed the chill from his eyes. The corner of his hand rasped against a patch of stubble he had missed when he shaved that morning.

'And what did Frank and Nora see this afternoon?' Denis went on.

Jonathan started. His eyes narrowed. 'Yes,' he said inquiringly, 'what did you see, Miss Morris? And you, young man — tell us what you saw.'

Frank told them calmly and succinctly, as though relating a tale about somebody else. His quietness and self-control carried a conviction of their own, despite the fantastic nature of the whole affair. When he had finished, there was silence.

Jonathan was the first to speak. He said: 'What conclusions do you draw from your truly remarkable experience?'

'None,' said Frank, 'as yet.'

'Except,' said Nora, 'that it ties up in some way with what you showed me from the passage window. The castle was the

164

same. And the creature or creatures inside
— or things, those horrors — '

'You're speaking of your future masters, dear young lady. Be more respectful.'

Denis slapped himself on the knee. His
father surveyed him reproachfully. Denis
said: 'Come on, tell us what's up your
sleeve.'

Jonathan crossed his legs and his eyes
wandered around the tense little semi-
circle. They were all waiting for him to
begin, and he enjoyed his moment of
power, though it was marred when he
looked at Simon.

'Go on,' said Simon coolly. 'We're
waiting for you.'

'I suppose you think you know it all,
already?'

'Not all of it,' said Simon; 'just a part.
Go ahead.'

Nora was not in the kitchen, but in the
cinema. It was four or five years ago, a
winter evening, when she had walked
down alone to the cinema that was
cramped in between the garage and the
stained, faded Wesleyan chapel. A horror
film — a ridiculous thing full of creeping

shadows, hand reaching from corners, contorted faces and screams, all backed up by muttering music . . . and Nora, who had gone there only because of the depression brought on by an accumulation of damp, miserable evenings behind her and the prospect of many more to come, shivered in her seat. It was nonsense, it was only a film, and even if it had been serious it would have lost much of its effect because of the catcalls and raucous comments of the usual gang of youths clustered at the back of the poky little hall. But it was frightening, nevertheless. Even though she knew it was a shadow play, Nora was scared to the pit of her stomach by the gradual approach of the gruesome climax. She knew, at the back of her mind, that she had to face that long walk back home, between rows of sinister shapes leering out from the dark trees with great phantasms of abomination stooping out of the skies . . .

Waiting, with her heart beating painfully.

This time it was no film, but reality.

Jonathan said: 'It's hard to know where

to begin. It really starts a long way back — so far back that I couldn't make it clear to you. Not easy to know how to explain why — and in any case,' he said with a sudden defiance, 'why should I pass on my information?'

He seemed aghast at his own folly. He opened and shut his mouth, and then settled in his chair and folded his arms.

'Why should I tell you? Foolish of me: I nearly allowed my vanity to run away with me. A bad failing. You'd like to know how much I know, wouldn't you?'

He was addressing Simon, who inclined his head. 'I admit,' he said without rancour, 'that I was hoping to hear your version of it. It would have filled in the pieces that are unfortunately missing from my own picture. Congratulations on your restraint: you have more self-control than I thought, Mr. Jonathan.'

'I'll get it out of him,' said Denis, making a lunge forward.

He did not get far. Simon's arm shot out and restrained him. They leaned at a precarious angle for a moment, then Simon forced Denis gently backwards.

'Don't be rash,' he said. 'This little man is an upstart, but he has certain talents. He wouldn't be sitting there smirking like that if he didn't feel that he could cope with most of us.'

'With all of you,' said Jonathan.

Simon's eyebrows lifted slightly. 'You don't know where I come into this.' And he repeated the question he had asked earlier: 'How did I get here, Mr. Jonathan?'

Jonathan now had himself well in hand. He made no reply, and showed no emotion. Simon smiled.

'Since our visiting expert won't let us into his secrets,' he said, 'I'll do my best to outline for you the story of what has led up to this night — '

'Stop! I won't let you tell these fools — '

'In order to finish what you have begun,' said Simon, 'you will need the help of someone here. Don't antagonise them too much. It will do them no harm to know what is being done.'

Jonathan, undecided, tried to weigh him up. While he was still pondering,

Simon continued.

'This is a crucial night in the history of the human race. Tonight the threads are all gathered up. Scattered and lost in uncounted centuries, they are now ready to be brought together once more — or so our friend here thinks. We are back at the gate, and the gate is open. The seal is broken, and all that we need now is the body through which the dark glory is to be made manifest. Am I right, most learned adept?'

Jonathan said curtly: 'Go on.'

'Long ago,' said Simon equably, 'when the first civilised men, not so long born of the slime and chaos of the earth's creation, made their first cities and put their years of barbarism behind them, establishing a precarious dominion over the still turbulent, shifting land and water, strange gods were shaped in the cold outer spaces. Out beyond the most distant stars, yet in their many-folded dimension close to everywhere in the ever-circling, ever-closed universe, wild spasms of immortality came into being and went seeking worlds that called to them, across space in search of what would assuage their thirst. They enmeshed Betelgeuse and wove their webs around Andromeda. They reached out for the loneliest stars on the edge of infinity, and hungered for the tiniest planet where sentient beings, with pride and hatred and lust blooming in their adventurous bodies, could play their part in feeding the gluttonous appetites of these all-pervading, groping gods.' He nodded. 'For gods they were: they were in all places, and yet in no place.'

'They devoured,' said Jonathan with an uncontrolled outburst of excitement. 'They engulfed, devoured and ravaged. Their dominion was absolute.'

'And their priests were all-powerful,' said Simon. 'You fancy yourself as a priest of the Atlantean gods, don't you, little fellow? They held in their hands the destinies of all men. On their altars were decided all problems of statecraft, and the laws were made in their reeking temples when the sacrifice smoke was thick and dark.'

'The fools let it slip. That must never happen again.'

'It will require someone more skilled than yourself to avoid such a catastrophe.' Simon looked at Jonathan, and then at the others, but he did not see them: he was staring into a world far beyond, addressing himself to unresponsive space. 'There was Atlantis, built on shifting sand but held miraculously stable by the arts of the Black Adepts. The blood flowed and cries rang through the temples as men and women died in agony . . . but the shapeless gods, encircling the world and yet living in human bodies when they so chose, permeating every soul, were satisfied, and the cities were held erect in triumph while still the land heaved and changed. Music, painting and poetry flourished. Wild hymns were sung to the sky, and the sky itself responded. The earth was sweet and new, and the sensual gods projected themselves into human bodies, revelling in the joys of this fresh, sparkling morning of mankind and tasting all the pleasure that was to be tasted when the world was young. They destroyed when it gave them pleasure to destroy, and they devised rituals of torment for their own entertainment, often evolving the details while, in their human forms, they lay in a lovers' embrace.'

Jonathan's eyes were shining. 'There were gods in those days. The gods will come back, and the faithfully devoted few will be rewarded.'

'They were vengeful gods,' said Simon. 'Do you think they'll be pleased to have the gate opened to them by a charlatan? Do you really think they will exalt you, Mr. Jonathan — will you be a high priest?'

Frank stirred restlessly. He said: 'Where are they — these beings — now? Or did they die when Atlantis was engulfed in a great flood, as I believe it was supposed to be?'

'There is no death for such as these. There is defeat and there is banishment to the cold wastes beyond Lyomoria, but there is no death. They are waiting.

'The priests became lax, and the gods became lazy, glutted with their own pleasures: that was the cause of their downfall. There was whispering in the courts, and plots to overthrow the priests began. The gods had come too close to the people who worshipped them, and did not understand the danger in which they walked. They thought revolt was out of the question. They relied on awe and fear, but the familiarity of having them mingling with the common crowd in the pursuit of animal pleasures drove out awe, and the plotting began. Slowly at first. If plans to lock the gods out of the fair, infinitely pleasurable world came to light, there were great orgies of sacrifice and punishment, but the plans came bubbling up again. The gods, it was murmured, were not all-powerful. They were immortal, incarnate spirits of evil, but they were not sacred beings; they could be attacked. There were men who said that all human beings should be treated with respect and intelligence, and that men should govern themselves instead of submitting to the dictates of wanton immortals and their arrogant priests. And in secret, slowly and with many reverses, young men trained for the battle that was to come. Ordinary weapons were useless. This was to be a spiritual conflict, as violent and destructive as the upheavals of the country about their cities. The White Adepts trained, evolving a magic that would defeat the very founders of Magic. It was a long task. All their work had to be done surreptitiously, with infinite care, for any slip at the last moment would ruin all that had gone before.

'You don't understand all this: I can see in your faces that it is too remote for you to grasp. But it was one of the decisive battles of the world, when it came. These men — and women — trained and worked in what was far worse than any enemy country in modern times. They sought to overthrow what they conceived to be an inexcusable tyranny, and for the work they succeeded in doing, even the most devoted adherents of the dark gods — even Jonathan, shall we say? — must feel admiration. It was so terrific a conflict that even today its fame has not altogether died. In garbled but recognisable versions, its memory is alive: some call it the battle of Moytura, others have no name for it, but associate it vaguely with the Christian stories of driving out devils, and those supposedly fanciful tales of driving out the old gods of the fields and trees; all myths of early Christian apostles driving out local spirits are merely variations on this much more ancient theme. And the Seal of Solomon — what is that but the symbolic expression of that last great curse that shattered the resistance of the gods, shattered many of them so that they were as though they had never been, and then drove them out and sealed the gateway? There they lie in Fomoria, or Lyomoria, or on the frozen plains of Yagrath . . . call it what you will.'

'They're gone, then,' said Denis inadequately.

'They are ready to return,' countered Jonathan.

Simon studied his finger-nails. He was curiously like a cat playing coolly and in leisurely fashion with a mouse. 'And you're going to call them?'

'I am,' said Jonathan. 'Can you stop me?'

'Frankly, I don't know.'

Nora cleared her throat. Even then, she had difficulty in speaking. At last she said:

'Where do the books come into this? The books have something to do with it.'

'They're the pieces of the jigsaw,' said Simon.

'Of which you lack an essential corner,' said Jonathan.

Simon again inclined his head. He was unruffled.

'The books,' he explained to his bewildered audience, 'provide the only key to that gate. It was not to be expected that all the gods should be expelled in one great body. There were strays who escaped the great defeat — cowards who had not pitted themselves against the White Adepts at the final conflict, and a few cunning spirits who had hidden away in case of need. They could not hide for long: they were sought out and dissolved in light — exorcised, if you prefer the word — but not before they had hurriedly prepared and disseminated the records of their most sacred rites. These manuscripts were hidden and passed on to a small group of devotees who still lived and remained true to the old faith. The White Adepts could seek out their enemy adepts, but ordinary people who retained their old beliefs were harder to distinguish — they did not emit psychic radiations in the same way as the magic fraternity did. They kept quiet, and the books were handed on. But they were scattered. It was impossible for the different groups of secret worshippers to meet: they were not sure of one another's whereabouts, and it would have been fatal to attempt to make any contact. There were several little cliques, each possessing valuable documents and arcane knowledge that was useless on its own, but that, fitted together by one who had studied and acquired the occult powers necessary to use the knowledge . . .

'For centuries the search has gone on. Atlantis fell, and mankind relapsed into barbarism, but descendants of Atlantis who had escaped while there was yet time treasured the last remnants of their black civilisation. Now it was possible to make more open attempts to join up with one another. But there were oceans to be crossed, and new, unfamiliar land masses to be explored. Generations — centuries, even — before there was any hope. It has been easier in recent years: there is no great opposition offered to students of the Black Arts, who may disguise their interests under a thousand different names; the last vestiges of the early laws, aimed at stamping out those who would call back the dark gods, were destroyed when the witchcraft laws, puny and trifling as they were, were repealed. Since then, it has been comparatively easy for the Black Adepts to make progress — '

'Not so very easy,' said Jonathan indignantly, as though his own brilliance were being impugned. 'It was hard to trace the families who held the records — the descendants of the original Atlantean devotees — and when they were traced, they might have died out, or accidents had caused books to go astray. Sometimes the books could not be read because of the abstruseness of the almost forgotten language.'

'But at least there was no need for

secrecy,' Simon pursued. 'There was no need for that crippling stealth that had held them back in the old days. They could not openly declare their intentions, but they could give their intentions another name, and by judicious advertising and propaganda hope that their fellows would realise the message that was being sent out and would get in touch with them. Across the wastes of the past, their families had handed down the secrets of the ancient lore, knowing that some day all the threads would be gathered together. When the old documents crumbled and the language of Atlantis was forgotten, new books were prepared. Great libraries of forbidden knowledge were amassed, new treatises were written — some of them flaunted in the face of the uncomprehending general public — and the training of adepts went on. There were persecutions and massacres, to be sure, but none of the later persecutors had the power of the White Adepts.'

'What happened to the White Adepts, anyway?' demanded Frank.

'They destroyed Atlantis,' said Jonathan venomously.

'They destroyed Atlantis,' Simon agreed. 'When the great upheaval shook the earth, and the flood waters rose, there were no dark gods to appeal to. The men of earth were alone, and although they fought with all the power they possessed, all the skill they had acquired through the long years, calling upon all the spiritual resources at their disposal, they were but mortal, and they could not maintain the equilibrium of Atlantis. Atlantis had been raised and upheld by evil. Certain warped bargains had been struck with black entities outside our normal space limits, and only by the blood of sacrifice and the strength drawn by adepts from hideous rites was the country made safe. There were natural laws, as it were: break them, as the rebellious White Adepts had broken them, and you had to take the consequences. A short spell of glorious freedom and social reform — and then the new Atlantis, the beautiful Lyonesse, was no more. Sustained by evil, it collapsed when the conditions of its existence were not fulfilled. Many escaped from the land, to South America, Egypt and lands that have themselves ceased to exist. From that day to this, the scattered families of the old belief have been endeavouring to establish contact with one another. From the number that slunk away before the floods came, it would seem that they knew what would happen — indeed, it's not unreasonable to suppose that they had a hand in the destruction. Possibly they knew enough to drown Atlantis.

'The dark gods were not fools. They knew that after many centuries the human race would grow lax once more, and then it would be possible to open the gateway to let them back into their Eden. A chosen man, a member of one of the families of adepts, would, it was prophesied, someday come and destroy the seal, offering the body of a human being as the pathway that is necessary to establish contact between that world and this, and the gods would return.

'Their influence has remained. When have the witches and warlocks ever been entirely stamped out?'

'The alchemist and sorcerer,' said

Jonathan, 'the spirits that ride the wind . . . strange powers, the blessed communicants at the Walpurgisnacht Sabbath . . . '

'One could almost believe that the gods have reached out, stretching tentative fingers through the veil that separates them from us, and imbued their faithful adherents with some of their own craft. They have not been forgotten. Half-consciously, in some cases, men have advanced along the road leading to the gateway through which the gods were expelled.

'And that gateway, as I discovered when I first opened your book-case, is through the castle on the hill.'

They had been expecting this, so that it came as no surprise. Nora began to surmise wildly what she and Frank had stepped into when they passed through the old arch in the castle. And why, if it was open, no-one came through . . . and why, apparently, there had been no opposition to the black magicians when they sought to gather up the scattered documents — and how so many of the evil books came to be in this farmhouse . . .

She said: 'How did all the books come to be here?'

'And what happened to the White Adepts?' Frank repeated. 'Did they leave no descendants?'

'One at a time, please,' said Simon. 'The books formed the library of one of the families I referred to. But there must have been a couple of unexpected deaths, and the knowledge was not handed on as it should have been. It was fortunate for the seekers that the library was not split up. By some freak of fortune it remained here. All trace of the place was lost until Mr. Jonathan here, who claims to be a member of the same family, found his way here by chance, or following up some hint he discovered in one of the books he himself possessed. A long chance, this discovery — but it has taken centuries for this one lucky chance to occur. The books here, as I discovered, make it clear that this is the place where the rites must be performed to recall the gods. The books which have been handed down to Mr. Jonathan tell how these rites must be performed. The place . . . and the ritual:

how many generations have passed away into the dust while men have struggled to bring those two essential things together? The dark gods have waited a long time for your arrival, Mr. Jonathan. They have waited for the day when their black record could be forgotten, and when the world was ready for their return — and now, here you are, claiming to be the Black Adept who is spiritually fitted to open the gate and welcome home your lords and masters.'

'I'm not just claiming to be an adept,' said Jonathan. 'I've worked it all out . . . no possibility of mistake. The way these things came into my hands, now — coincidence, you think? This is destiny. I'm descended from the original families, I've mixed with the secret societies, I know all that must be done — '

'Are you sure? Are you positive you've got it all under control?'

Frank persisted: 'What about the White Adepts?'

'That's what's worrying Mr. Jonathan,' Simon smiled. 'He doesn't know. Nobody ever knows. What about the White

Adepts? That has always been the question. When Atlantis died, so many of them were drowned, but they had great powers, despite their inability to prevent the catastrophe, and it is inconceivable that they should have passed away entirely. At one time and another, when the Black Adepts have flourished and shown signs of becoming powerful once more, there have been signs that the White Adepts were not absent. They have been baffling. Time and again they have suddenly, inexplicably appeared and thwarted Black Adepts who thought themselves on the verge of great discoveries. At crucial moments there have been strange setbacks. There has been a continuous, unrelenting struggle for the books — but the White Ones have never been so obvious as their enemies. No-one can trace the reason for their appearances and disappearances. They have been a disturbing, unknown factor. One can never tell when they will make their influence felt — can one, Mr. Jonathan?'

Jonathan scowled.

'It has always been the main obstacle,' Simon went on. 'They are elusive spirits, these White Adepts. So far they have not let their enemies outwit them — '

'This time they'll be too late,' sneered Jonathan.

'Is it any good my warning you what a risk you're running? Not only the chance of encountering the White Ones, but the fact that you may experience some — er, difficulty — with those you are hoping to call up. You claim to be an adept, but I refuse to believe it — '

'I — '

'You're meddling with something far too great for your puny talents. Knowledge of the commonplace magic of earth will not help you to handle these beings who come through the gate. Have you any conception of what you might loose on the world? Do you imagine that what you have gleaned from the books that have, by a strange chance, come into your possession, will enable you to control these restless immortals who have waited so long? Think, man, before it's too late.'

Jonathan grinned back at him. 'I'm confident enough. No doubts at all. The gate is open.'

'Before you go any further with the rite, tell me what it entails. Tell me what you're going to perform, so that — '

'Do you really think I would? Not me, youngster. This is what I've been working up to for years . . . fulfilment, this is. You can't spoil it, and I don't care who you are. It's too late this time. What I've started can't be halted now.'

'Nor can it be continued,' said Simon, 'without an assistant.'

Mrs. Morris leaned forward to poke the fire. Her attention had been wandering; she accepted the fact that they — and, indeed, the whole world, by the sound of it — were in danger, but she could not grasp the details, and found consolation in making short, angry jabs with the poker through the bars of the grate. The coals shuffled and flame licked up. A smell of pitch arose from one lump that was emitting a thin, violent jet of grey smoke.

Jonathan said: 'Yes, I need an assistant. You'd better make up your minds who it's to be. Willing or unwilling — I don't mind.'

'Then you ought to,' said Simon. 'You know quite well you're running a terrible risk if you use an unwilling, untrained helper. It should be an adept, really.'

'Are you volunteering, then?'

'I am not.'

Jonathan stood up. He seemed to feel more assurance when he was above them.

'To carry out the ritual,' he said importantly, 'I need a human being who will surrender himself or herself to my spiritual control. Physical contact is necessary before the gods can return to earth — '

'A sacrifice!' said Frank.

'No, young man. Nothing to fear, I assure you.' He glanced apprehensively at Simon, but Simon remained quiet. 'I'm asking for your help,' Jonathan proceeded. 'I'll be frank. If I don't get it willingly, I'll force someone to help me.'

'The risk — '

'The risk dosen't count. I know enough to overcome any danger. We can't hold back now. Well . . . ? I'm asking for your help: it's a real privilege I'm offering you.'

He sounded like a conjurer asking for a

watch or a pack of cards. There was no response.

'No offers?' said Simon jocularly. 'Mr. Jonathan can't perform his miracles without some help, you know. The vibrant force of a human being is necessary before the ritual can be carried out. It's on much the same lines as a seance: visions can only appear when there is a medium present — preferably a medium with the ability to produce ectoplasmic phenomena. There must be this human reservoir on which to draw. That's what Jonathan is asking for, in his own friendly way.'

The fire spluttered. They all sat still.

Nora stared in front of her, incredulous. This was real. She might blink, make surreptitious movements, and pinch herself, but nothing would shake the solid, convincing scene before her. This was real.

'Since there's no reply,' said Jonathan, 'we'll have to try the other way.'

Denis launched himself from his chair.

Simon cried out, but he was too late. Denis seemed to reel against Jonathan, then he clutched at his head and was thrown backwards, although Jonathan had done no more than raise his right hand sharply. Frank caught Denis as he staggered, and lowered him back into his chair, pale and shaking.

'Don't try that sort of game,' said Jonathan, glancing at Simon to see how he was taking this display of ability.

Simon said: 'Well, what are you going to do?'

'The word seance strikes a chord,' said Jonathan pleasantly. 'There's a little ritual . . . Yes, I think that a tranquil soul would be a good thing, for all of us. Since I must take possession by force — '

'So you're hoping to do it *that* way?' said Simon thoughtfully.

'You know what I am proposing?'

'Very well. Yes, I know it very well.'

Nora appealed to Simon with an instinctive gesture. He made no reply, but he did not seem worried, and she felt a stir of hope.

'Let's make preparations,' said Jonathan, striking the back of the chair nearest to him, and making Mr. Morris jump violently. 'The time is short. We must lower the light . . . and we'll have no more stupid assaults on me, if you please. I can make the results more unpleasant: I refrained this time because' — significantly — 'I thought our young friend might be useful. One can never tell: he may be the one.'

Nora continued to stare at Simon. Slowly he became aware of her rapt attention, and smiled reassuringly at her.

She said: 'Shall we — ?'

'We'll go ahead as Mr. Jonathan wishes,' said Simon. 'It will be best that way.'

She could not tell if he spoke confidently or with dull resignation.

10

The wick was turned down. The lamp plopped twice like a flashing light-house and then went out. Jonathan, arranging chairs to his satisfaction, smiled. 'Thank you.' The firelight flickered on his face — too grimly appropriate, thought Nora.

She felt that they were not the only people in the room. There were others, crowding about them, filling the room with a surge of unnatural life. The impression was so overpowering that when someone touched her arm she had difficulty in stifling a whimper.

'You're very jumpy,' said Simon.

The touch of his hand on her arm became strangely comforting.

'Are you sure this is all right?' she asked in a low voice. 'I don't know what it's all leading up to, but are you sure you can handle it?'

'This is the only way.' They stood back as Jonathan completed the circle of chairs and dusted his hands smugly. 'There would have to be a fight between us sooner or later: I prefer to get it over now. We shall each draw on reserves of which we know, and . . . ' He pursed his lips. 'Well, we shall see. There's no way of avoiding it.'

Jonathan stood in the centre of the circle and waved his hand invitingly towards the chairs. 'Are you ready, ladies and gentlemen?'

'Just like Christmas,' said Denis. He still moved weakly and uncertainly, like someone recovering from a violent electric shock.

They sat down.

'In order to maintain the Christmas spirit,' said Jonathan ironically, 'will you please hold hands? It is necessary to establish an unbroken chain. And let me warn you not to break it or to attempt any foolishness. I can deal with all of you if needs be. Let's be sociable about it. Young Simon will tell you that this is a dangerous ritual: any attempt you make on my life will inevitably result in the loss of your own — and almost certainly the lives of your friends also.'

Nora was holding Simon's left hand and Frank's right hand. Frank was tense, but Simon did not seem to be worried. She stared straight ahead. Someone would start talking in a minute — about an operation, wasn't it? They would say, 'Here's the patient's eye,' and put a wet gooseberry in your hand, and so it would go on. Then she noticed her mother taking Jonathan's hand with an involuntary shudder, and said:

'Change places with me . . . '

Simon's hand pressed hers.

Mrs. Morris said: 'There's quite comfy I am, Nora.' She was afraid, but she refused to show it. Nora turned to Simon, trying to make him understand how dangerous it was: her mother was next to Jonathan, and . . . ? Simon shook his head.

'Can we settle down?' said Jonathan pleasantly.

There was silence save for the spasmodic hiccupping of the fire. Denis shuffled his feet once. Frank's hand became warm; Simon's still lay motionless.

Jonathan's head fell slightly forward and his eyes began to close, but Nora was sure that he still knew all that might happen about him. He was not defence-less; she glanced warningly at her brother, who was holding Jonathan's left hand and might conceivably be planning some misguided ju-jitsu effort. Denis, however, was looking down at the floor, his toes lined up with a crack in the tiles.

The room became more and more oppressive, and they all became aware of an unaccountable activity, a frenzied coming and going. Nora wanted to turn her head, sure that someone stood behind her, but there was no sign of movement close to anyone else's chair, so why should there be any behind hers? She kept still, listening to Jonathan's harsh breathing and the intermittent creaking of one of the chairs. It was the chair with the loose rung. Who was sitting on it? As soon as she tried to locate it, the squeaks seemed to come from every direction, and the rustle of unseen beings intensified.

Jonathan's head fell forward on his chest, but he was still taut and responsive.

Nora felt Simon twitch slightly, and saw that he had his eyes closed — or was it the effect of the shadows that rose from about his chair and covered his face with a swaying veil?

The waiting was unbearable. The ticking of the clock became a steady pounding and then faltered; she heard it wheezing and producing noises she had never heard before, as though it could no longer force itself to rap out the time. Jonathan was still. Her father, she saw, trying to make a comforting joke out of the familiar sight, was falling off to sleep. Her own eyes felt heavy. It was surprisingly comforting to shut them, cutting out the smudged, flickering vision of the room . . . and then she opened them again, and but for the firm clasp of Frank's hand and Simon's light but compelling touch, she would have rubbed them to wakefulness. Perhaps sleep was what Jonathan was trying to will upon her, or upon any of them: perhaps he was waiting for one of them to nod and to fall asleep, so that he could take possession. Her father's drowsiness ceased to be a subject of even the mildest would-be amusement.

Without warning, a lump of coal in the grate split and fell apart, pieces rattling into the fender and a flame leaping up to shine with crimson laughter in the face of Jonathan. Then it died, and the unseen beings came back from the crowded corners, whispering and jostling, urging, complaining, setting the air quivering with notes outside the human range.

And as Nora clenched her teeth and decided to pull her hands free, to stand up and shout out any nonsense at all that would break the iron circle of their mute imprisonment, Jonathan began to speak.

He said: 'There is a voice crying out across the frozen plain. Come closer. This is your servant, and here is your chalice of fulfilment.' Then he muttered something unintelligible.

At once the sense of being watched deserted Nora, and it was as though a cloud of hovering birds had drifted over Jonathan's chair. He raised his head, and his face was contorted.

'Shall we choose?'

The room throbbed to the beating of eager wings.

Simon made a brief noise in his throat.

'This is the hour of the choice,' said Jonathan. 'Lend me your powers. Reach out from the cold wastes beyond Yagrath and infuse me with the spirit that will bind a mortal to me until I lay him at your feet. Tonight we choose the opener of the way. In the morning, when day is born, the gateway shall be flung wide.'

He lifted his arms as high as he could, holding up those of his neighbours, like an ancient prophet crying out. There was a rushing wave of cold that splashed bitterly into the room, an intense cold that dragged at the breath and gnawed with vicious rapidity into the stomach.

'This is the wind of the coldest of hells,' said an unexpected voice. Nora, tightening her grasp, realised that Simon was speaking.

Jonathan's eyelids flickered for a moment, and there was a vague stirring in the air.

Simon said: 'Is it, then, for a puny dilettante to command the lords of darkness? Is it a sound of rejoicing I hear, or the hollow laughter of mockery?'

There was some force gathering its strength within him. The two adversaries faced one another across the small circle of tiled floor.

'I call on the lords of Annwn,' cried Jonathan, 'on the riders of the wind, the dogs of — '

Simon's laugh cut him short. 'Can you appeal no higher than that? What of those who are masters of the lords of Annwn? What of . . . ' He uttered a name that was like no name Nora had ever heard. It was not a sound of normal speech; it was not a word, but a cry. It thrummed reverberatingly, and was roared triumphantly back by the echoes. Jonathan cowered away.

'To know the name,' said Simon, 'is to hold power in one's fingers.'

Jonathan spat a short sentence at him, and once more it was as though unseen forces met above their heads in the clash of tortured conflict.

This, then, was the battle Simon had foretold. Jonathan was savage, holding back his enemy with sharp, angry blows, while Simon mocked and seemed to be playing.

'There was a day long ago,' he began calmly, addressing them all as though this were a normal conversation, but not letting go of his neighbours' hands, 'when Owain Glyndwr swept the English across Wales. It was a typical campaign of its kind, but there were times when it was thought that he could actually banish the conquerors from his country forever, and behind the red dragon came not only the patriots and warriors, but many priests and devotees of old secret religions, believing that the day was at hand when they could establish at least a form of the old worship. There were many hopeful hearts in those days. And none was more hopeful than one Llewelyn the Black, son of an unknown father and a mother who was known to be a witch. He was one of the Adepts, a great man among the faithful children of the cults that had for so long been driven underground. He was old, and afraid that death would come riding behind him before he saw even the first sign of the great rebirth of which all like him had dreamed for so long. And then, along with the straggling but victorious men of Glyndwr, this tired adept came to the castle.

'It was not a ruin then, but a stronghold from which the English had been dislodged only at a heavy price. There were legends about the castle; no-one could say how old it was; but no-one asked many questions, for it was a splendid watch-tower, commanding so much of the countryside from which reprisals might be expected. The soldiers were thankful for shelter, and the Black Adept was thankful that his footsteps had been directed to this place while his powers were still strong. For he recognised the arch, as it had been described to him. He said the prescribed words of homage before it, and the stir of acknowledgment confirmed that this was indeed the place. He rejoiced, and sought out his followers, and chose from them a willing disciple who would give his body over to the impatient gods so that contact might be established. This, they said, explaining away their personal lusts and anticipation of reward by a plea of patriotism, this will mean victory for the Welsh cause. With the help of the great old gods, Glyndwr might be nominally ruler of the world. It was a mad, lustful dream, but it seemed so easily attainable. All the old manuscripts had not yet been recovered, but they knew many incantations that had been passed down from father to son, and they felt that the gods would help them to achieve their liberation.

'But they made errors. The world was not yet ready, and the spells were not strong enough. The gateway was neither open nor shut. All the words had not been said, and the great seal was not shattered. The triumphal return was not accomplished. For one night there was a lunatic jarring and twisting of dimensions and planes of being, and hideous distortions were seen in the land. The furious gods, whirled into this disruptive confusion, reached out savagely for the unsuccessful adept and his miserable assistant, and drew them through into that icy world from which they themselves were unable to escape. The adept had blundered, and perhaps in his impatience held back the day when release would at last be achieved. For whenever such an upheaval of cosmic forces took place, there was always the danger that the slumbering White Ones would reappear to break up the association of adepts, making it necessary to begin all over again the slow process of collecting information and establishing contact with other groups. There has always been grave danger when bunglers have tried their hand at calling back the old gods.'

Jonathan sat immobile, his arms still held above his head. His lips began to move, formulating some new curse or some fresh appeal to the power that drove him on, but before he could start, a new voice began to speak, in a pleasant, unhurried manner, like an elderly man telling a simple, attractive fairy tale.

'There was a Sabbath when all the adepts, sorcerers, alchemists, witches and their familiars in Hungary met on a great plain and built the ceremonial fires.'

Nora could not tell whether this was Simon still speaking. The words seemed to come from the centre of the circle, each one falling with the crystal sound of a stone dropping into a pool.

'It was a splendid occasion, for only recently many families of the old belief had found one another, and had pooled their knowledge. They did not know where the original gateway was, for that particular manuscript had not come into their possession, but they talked among themselves and decided that the gateway was now no more than a symbol. It must have crumbled before this, they argued, and to speak in terms of 'the gateway' was to speak symbolically. The gateway, said the wise, well-read adepts, excited by the revelry going on about them on this night of magnificent debauchery, is only an expression: the gateway really exists anywhere and everywhere, and the rites of which we are the most skilled practitioners will open it. Then there will be jubilation!

'The lesser magicians and the witches

made carnival that night. They crouched over their fires and they rode the wind, so that there was no stillness in that part of the country, and the bravest men locked their doors and prayed for dawn.

'But at dawn, as it was commanded in the books of old wisdom, the greatest of all rituals was to take place. With the dawn of a new day would come the birth of a new era, when old splendours should be renewed and great benefits reaped by those who had been faithful for so long.

'So very, very long . . . Was this indeed the day of the great release?

'There was a night of preparation, during which certain of the adepts also indulged in the sensual pleasures that were to be found wherever they sought them. Disturbing music was played by musicians who were nowhere to be seen, and at intervals men and women clustered about smoking fires and chuckled bloodily at what they were doing. Soon the sky would begin to lighten, and then this great assembly of chosen families and their supporters would take part in the recall of their true masters.

'All this we know, for it is written in the records. What came after is but imperfectly described in the records: there would appear to have been some confusion.'

Simon was leaning forward, tense and, one would have said, puzzled.

Jonathan said, in an awed tone: 'This is the tale of the Great Destruction — '

'The Great Destruction,' agreed the gentle, urbane voice. 'For there was a battle, a great clash of White and Black Adepts that filled the air with a clamour of anguish and a great flame of dissolution, burning more brightly than the morning that touched the skies in the east. No-one knew how the White Adepts came to this accursed spot; no-one had heard of them for many years, and it was not known where they slept. But somehow — as it has always been and always will be — they awoke from their watchful sleep when they knew that evil was massing its legions in one place, where it might easily be smitten. Preparations were being made to carry out a damnable infamy; such preparations make a psychic disturbance that is like the sound of a warning trumpet to the White Adepts, who are everywhere, not to be escaped or deceived. When the situation warrants it, they can strike — '

'But they're not always successful,' snarled Jonathan. 'So far the ritual has not been carried out correctly. There have been mistakes. But what of the time when no mistakes are made? What defence can be put up then: what can be done in the hour — it's close enough now! — when the gods are really recalled . . . what then? Another battle? The result . . . '

The voice laughed agreeably. 'Another battle. Yes, there will be that. It may be that the White Adepts will be defeated this time; it may be that they cannot hope to vanquish evil in the end, despite the great hopes and prophecies. If they are wrong, blackness will triumph despite all efforts, and the great Day of Judgment will be a hideous shambles. No-one can say. But the White Adepts will fight: they will fight as they fought at Moytura, at the Pyramid, of Tarol and in other distant universes that are not known on this tiny globe. They have become more than man, but they have not deserted man, and they can be recalled. As they came in a ball of light across the outer spaces to join combat and shatter the black ones in what you call the Great Destruction, so they may come again. They will ride in consuming fire and throw against the leagues of darkness all the glory of light. The gods of Atlantis have been banished, and it were better that the whole universe should be torn apart than that they should return. But then again' — with an endearing chuckle that Nora unaccountably seemed to recognise — 'it might not even be necessary for the White Adepts to intervene. A charlatan might easily encompass his own destruction without any outside assistance. Just one small blunder — '

Jonathan's courage was quickly returning. He said, arrogantly: 'There's no charlatanry here. Things are going to happen — make no mistake about it.'

The fire was dying down and the light became dull red.

'Very well,' came the reply; 'but have no

illusions — if the call comes, it will be answered. As Arthur sleeps in Avalon, and the blessed knights keep watch in Caer Sidi for the day when there shall be need of them, so the White Adepts keep watch. Make no mistake, indeed . . . '

A pinpoint of light hung suddenly in the air at the centre of the circle. It grew and became more brilliant, and Nora felt Simon's nails biting into her palm. The red glow on Jonathan's twisted, evil face changed to a hard white radiance that caused him to squirm away like a rat from fire.

Then, somehow — the light was too intense and the sense of angry excitement too overpowering for Nora to be sure of the details — the circle was broken, and there was a shout of possessive rage. The light died, and a chair shrieked along the floor. Jonathan was chanting in a high rasping voice. Simon rose unsteadily to his feet. The soothing spell of the discursive voice was broken. For long, unaccountable seconds the climax of the spiritual tussle was fought out in the room, without physical movement on the

209

part of the antagonists, yet bearing agonisingly upon the nerves of the other members of the group.

The weight of the untranquil silence . . .

This is madness, thought Nora despairingly. I'm mad. We're all mad, and it will have to end soon. Something must break.

The ceiling was far above, its distant beams clouded, hung with writhing shapes.

Lunacy and evil . . .

The strain like the rising note of a siren. It can't keep on.

A violin string tuned up and up until it snaps.

The human reason, and its capacity — how great? — for sustaining the assault of warped unreason . . .

Not much more, thought Nora wildly.

The black shapes plunged . . .

Simon gave a hoarse gurgle and stepped forward, falling to his knees. Jonathan, still on his chair, emitted a long sigh. The struggle was over, and the stillness was like that of a deserted street after a violent political brawl. Only the faint but persistent smell of hatred remained.

Simon got up slowly and dusted himself down as though nothing of any consequence had happened. Nora looked up at him. Neither of the two men gave any inkling of the outcome of their struggle. Nora waited for Simon to speak.

Or for anyone to speak.

The ticking of the clock was audible again.

Jonathan said: 'It's done.' He spoke in a level voice.

'It's done,' agreed Simon. 'One of us has been chosen . . . is possessed.'

11

'You lost, then?' said Nora to Simon.

Mrs. Morris was lighting the lamp again and tut-tutting as she caught sight of the clock, and, by an automatic swift calculation, realised that the time was almost nine o'clock.

Denis poked the fire and felt for the coal shovel.

Frank came and stood beside Nora. He said: 'What went wrong?'

'Don't be despondent,' said Simon.

'Despondent? We want to know where we are. What happened when you fell on your knees? Were you giving in to Jonathan, or is it going to work out all right, or — '

'Someone in this room,' said Jonathan precisely, 'is possessed.'

Mrs. Morris cautiously turned the wick higher.

'Try and put it in simple words,' said Denis harshly, turning from the fire.

Simon said: 'Perhaps I'd better do it.

What friend Jonathan planned to do has been accomplished. One of us is completely under a spell — you can call it hypnosis, if you like, though it's deeper than that. In order to have an untroublesome human body to provide the earthly energy that will enable the gods to return, the adept must make use of one of us. That one of us has been chosen and claimed: that's what the struggle was about. One of us is no longer in possession of his or her full faculties — little more than a zombie, as a matter of fact.'

'Which one?' snapped Denis.

Jonathan laughed. 'You'd like to know.'

'There's no way of telling,' said Simon. 'It might be any of us. He — or she — will behave normally, speak and eat normally. From outside there will seem to be no change — '

Frank said: 'It could be you. Jonathan could be making you say these things.'

'It could be. Or you, for that matter.'

'I know it's not me.'

'That's what you're saying, but how are we to know?'

Denis took a step forward. 'I'm

prepared to bet on Frank being the same as he was,' he said. 'How can we tell it's not you, Simon?'

'You can't.'

'Bewildering, isn't it?' said Jonathan, with obvious relish.

Frank and Denis closed in on either side of Simon, moved by a common purpose. Jonathan said, with a swift change of mood: 'Stay where you are.'

Simon frowned. 'You seem very sure it's me, you two.'

'You're so damned cool about it,' said Denis suspiciously. 'We know you had some sort of fight with Jonathan, and that you lost — '

'Do you know I lost?'

'Well . . . '

'Because I admit someone in this room has been . . . taken over, shall we say? — because of that, have I necessarily lost? The game isn't played yet. In fact, it doesn't start for a few hours yet.'

Nora said impulsively: 'I think Simon's the same as he was before.'

Her brother's eyes narrowed. 'He himself says that there wouldn't be any change that you could detect,' he pointed out.

'All the same — '

'Who do you think it is, then? Me?'

'Don't be ridiculous, Denis.'

'Who, then?'

She realised how impossible it was. There was something about Simon that made it hard for her to believe he had been changed in any way — but that applied to all the rest of them equally. They were all as they had been from the beginning. She knew that Jonathan's eyes were fixed on her, and she turned angrily to him.

'Well?' he said.

'If you've hurt my mother, or my father . . . '

Mr. Morris started. He had already edged his chair back to the newly flickering fire. 'Eh?'

'Is it . . . ?'

'I'm not saying anything,' said Jonathan. 'But why worry? Whoever it is, the rest of you will come to no harm. This is no Frankenstein's monster, but a walking shadow of a being completely under control.'

'Yes,' said Frank; 'under *your* control.'

Jonathan adjusted his tie. 'It will do you no harm. As far as any of you are concerned, he — or she, as my young friend has pointed out — will be to all intents and purposes the same person as the one we knew earlier in the evening.'

Mrs. Morris said: 'We'll do the washin' up, Nora fach.'

Even as they went out, Nora was wondering whether her mother had been chosen. But was there any way of finding out? She knew all her mother's gestures, and so far had detected nothing unusual, but that meant nothing. She turned up the lamp fastened to the wall over the sink, and then said:

'The kettle.'

'There was some water in it. Hot it'll be in no time.'

They were not looking directly at one another.

Nora said: 'Mother . . . '

'The sooner we get this finished, the sooner we can go to bed, and tired I am tonight. No more talk after this, I'm thinkin'.'

'Are you all right?'

'Tired I am,' Mrs. Morris repeated.

'But apart from that — ?'

'Are you thinkin' I'm the one, then?'

They stood by the sink, both suspicious. She's not sure it's not me, thought Nora. She said:

'You think it's me, and I think it might be you. If we both think that way, it can't be either of us. I can see what you're thinking, and — '

'A clever way it might be to make me think . . . but of course it's one of the others. Though I don't know what's goin' on, anyway. Mad.'

Nora went to fetch the kettle from the rejuvenated fire, sensing the hostility in the room as she crossed it. They had been studying one another covertly, and now they turned their attention to her. Denis said, speculatively: 'Nora — '

'I'm busy,' she snapped back at him.

Back with her mother, she began to wonder again. It was all very well to say that someone else had been chosen, but when you were alone with someone, even engaged on such a mundane business as washing and drying crockery, you couldn't help feeling a nervous prickling over your scalp. There was a buzz of voices from the other side of the passage. What were they talking about now? Nora wanted to go to bed, yet she also wanted to watch what everyone else was doing. To separate now would be to invoke nightmares and nervous awakenings from sleep, hearing the creak of old boards, the sound of the wind under the roof, and the ceaseless chatter of noises that existed only in one's imagination, but did not prove any the less frightening because of that.

Mrs. Morris was apparently anxious to return to the other room. She was hurriedly mopping the drain-board and drying her hands before Nora had finished hanging the cups on their hooks.

'Cold in here.'

It was always cold in here in winter — why say such a thing now? It was not like her mother: was it a false note, an intimation that Jonathan's camouflage was not perfect? Nora automatically stepped away. Mrs. Morris sensed this sudden fear, and twisted round impatiently. 'Don't get yourself so jumpy, girl. Bad enough without jumps and shakings.'

'Who do you think it is?'

Mrs. Morris shook her head. 'It might be anyone.'

'Dad — '

'Be quiet.' The words were snapped out. Very convincing in their way, but . . .

They went back to the sullen group by the fire. Jonathan's crouching shape dominated the room, as menacing as a patient vulture.

'Welcome to Suspects' Corner,' said Frank.

'We're all sitting around asking questions and hoping someone will make a slip,' said Denis grimly. 'It's fun. Afterwards there'll be some forfeits.'

Simon said: 'You're wasting your time'

Mrs. Morris looked at the clock and yawned. 'For once,' she said defiantly, as though poking a lion through the bars of a cage just to see what would happen, 'it's early to bed for me. If anythin' happens, there's no use me interferin', so there's not long I'm going to stay down here. But I'd like to know when it'll be — whatever it is.'

She folded her hands across her apron

like a Crusader's effigy and surveyed them provocatively.

'Well, then?'

Frank favoured her with an admiring smile. 'If you're the zombie, Mrs. Morris, you're a very self-willed one. Personally, I'm crossing you off my black list.'

'That's not what I'm asking.' Mrs. Morris was not to be drawn. She asserted her position as mistress of the household, so proudly that even the dark spirits that clustered about the lonely farm buildings might well have been abashed.

Frank was right. This couldn't be a pretence, thought Nora.

'What about it?' Denis said to Jonathan. 'As Mum says, when will it be, whatever it is?'

'At dawn.'

'How appropriate. Do we all assemble in a reverent circle?'

'You won't find it any laughing matter,' said Jonathan. 'At the appointed time, the chosen human will be called, and the ritual will be carried out. You may all sleep. Won't do you any harm. There's nothing else you can do — this time there will be no mistakes. Get what rest you can: no-one will harm you during the night.'

'We accept your word for that, of course,' said Denis bitterly.

'If there's nothing to do, we're only wastin' time with this old talk,' said Mrs. Morris. 'Come on, Rhys. Give your dad a push, now.'

'Bed?' exclaimed Denis. 'Without any supper?'

'You don't want any,' his mother told him.

Nora's suspicions were aroused again. This was unlike her mother. Not even a cup of tea . . .

'With so much disorganisation, I don't think we ought to expect anything,' said Frank equably.

Denis said: 'You're being very obliging, mate.'

They eyed one another.

'For myself,' said Denis, 'I think I'd sooner stay up. I think we ought to stick around down here, so that if anything happens we know who's causing it. When the big bang comes, I want my eyes open.'

Simon said: 'It wouldn't be any good. Nothing will happen before dawn, and then we shall see whether Mr. Jonathan gets everything his own way. Personally, I propose to sleep down here, if Mrs. Morris doesn't object.'

'I could make up a bed for you in . . . '

'In Jonathan's room,' Denis finished for her. 'That's a smashing idea. Let them fight it out together.'

Simon bowed and smiled. 'Very kind of you. But if you've no objections, I'll settle in front of the fire. Please take my word for it that you'll be all right. Jonathan isn't going to get up to any mischief once you're asleep: he can't do anything until dawn. I promise you I'll be doing a lot of thinking between now and then.'

'How do we know you're capable of thinking at all?' asked Frank. 'You might be using words that Jonathan has put into your head right at this moment.'

'In which case you can sit up and watch me all night. You'll be very tired by the time morning comes, and very disappointed when you realise that it was time wasted. Believe me: nothing will happen until the time comes to call the — er — assistant.'

'And then what?'

'It won't be the end of the world,' said Jonathan persuasively. 'You'll all go on living . . . if you don't do anything foolish.'

'I have a feeling we recently fought a war about this sort of thing,' Denis said. 'Well, what about it? Do we all stay up, or do we go to bed?'

Nora said: 'I think we can trust Simon. I believe he knows what's going on. Let's go and get some sleep.'

When she had spoken, she wondered what her words meant. Had she dismissed the possibility of Simon being possessed? Cross off Simon, and her mother — and Frank . . . and Denis, who was her brother . . . but what had being her brother got to do with it? And there was no way of being sure about Simon, really.

There was so little hope of being sure of anything that they all accepted the hopeless position and turned to go to bed. Simon remained in the kitchen, assuring Mrs. Morris, who was not to be daunted, that he needed only a couple of blankets. For a few minutes the fire of her hospitality warmed the trembling house, and it was just as though a visitor were staying after an evening's enjoyment. The sensation did not last, and Nora hesitated as she and her mother stepped into the dark passage, the flame of the candle bending protestingly before the draught. A chill struck up from the floor. Nora glanced back, and saw Simon standing in front of the fire, his head bowed in thought. Simon was their only chance; Simon was the only one of them who knew what all this grotesque charade meant. She said:

'Simon, you'll try . . . ?'

It was impossible to formulate an expression that would say what she meant him to understand. 'You won't give up?' she appealed.

He started. She could not see his face.

'Get some rest,' he said gently. 'There's the whole night before us, and you've nothing to fear.'

He sat down on the edge of the couch that had been pulled out from behind the table for him, and she left him, wishing that they had all decided instead to stay in the room together. Perhaps there was no safety in numbers, but one felt more comfortable Her mother, walking ahead with the flickering candle, was a distorted, unfamiliar shape. The passage itself was a territory of nightmare, full of crouching things that had never been there before. Nora wanted to run along to the stairs and dash up them, away from the whispering fear that walked mockingly behind her, in her footsteps.

The light of the candle in her room was little comfort. It exaggerated the shapes of the furniture and seemed to retreat from advancing black fingers that tapped in the corners. The little webwork of cracks in one part of the ceiling took on the lineaments of a grinning face, and she could not find any angle from which it did not look the same. It had never been that way before, but now the grimace was set and could not be avoided.

The creaking of the window-frame and the swaying of the curtains were ordinary, everyday things that tonight clutched at her heart. The thought of blowing out the candle was terrifying, yet no less terrifying were the monsters its uncertain flame conjured up.

Next door there was a comforting buzz of voices. Her mother and father, arguing in their same half-hearted, inevitable way. The words were indistinct, but Nora could follow the general trend without difficulty. Mrs. Morris was already in bed, ready for sleep, but her husband was tossing and turning, complaining of feeling wide-awake; after dozing in his chair all day, he became restless at night, and would twist and turn — 'There's an ol' fidget he is,' Mrs. Morris would complain, and vow never to let him have any more naps during the day — and a steady little murmur of complaints would sound through the wall.

They, at any rate, were comforting in their adherence to routine.

Or, were they? Again, one could not be absolutely certain.

Nora, having nerved herself to the act of blowing out the candle, was brought up sharply by this sudden thought. Not for the first time to-day, it was as though the floor had been dissolved beneath her, leaving her to fall into depths she could not calculate.

Before she could hesitate further, she puffed, and the flame died to a little, red smouldering glow on the end of the wick. The smell of wax hung in the cold air for a minute as Nora felt her way across to the bed, and climbed in. At first the room was dark, then the shape of the window began to nudge its way through the blackness. The light was grey and indistinct, but as she lay and watched — wanting to look away, for she had a childish fear of what might happen at windows . . . whisking aside of curtains, unimaginable horrors — the grey was tinged with dull red. She dared not move. She saw, as though she had been standing by the window itself, the shape of the ruins, and at the same time the shape of a great bulk that was not a ruin. Her mother and father were silent. Further along, she thought she could hear a dull murmur of voices from Denis and Frank, but that might have been only the increasing moaning of the wind. And in any case, Denis and Frank were a long way away: too many steps for her to tread if anything should happen: she knew she would be trapped, her feet powerless as in nightmare, if anything really did happen. Besides, there was no telling whether Denis or Frank could be trusted. Someone in the house was a walking slave, a creature without will. Loneliness pressed in on her . . .

'I don't like this business of slinking off to bed,' said Denis.

'I feel tired enough, myself,' confessed Frank. 'Even downright terror gives way after a while. I couldn't have kept my eyes open much longer.'

'So long as that's not the idea.'

'What do you mean?'

Denis yawned. 'I'm not in much of a state myself, but I'm trying to keep going. If someone wants to lull us into a state of weariness — '

'That someone being Jonathan?'

'Yes. This may all be part of his plan. I don't want to go off to sleep if that's the idea. If Jonathan wants me to close my baby blue eyes, that's one good reason for keeping them open.'

'All night?'

Denis groaned. 'It's a tough proposition,' he admitted.

'What about taking watches?'

'I've been thinking that.'

They studied one another cautiously. Slowly a reluctant smile broke across Frank's face. He said: 'Are you thinking what I'm thinking?'

'I suppose I am.'

'We're both in the same position. One of us may be Mr. Jonathan's little offering to the gods. I know I'm not, but maybe you know you're not, too. Since we can't tell what's in the other bloke's mind, that helps neither of us. But there's no reason to suppose that this — this poor, possessed being — is going to be harmful. We've got to start somewhere, and I'm working on the supposition that there's no danger for any of us until dawn. We can't sit here and suspect one another all night long. So the best thing to do is to decide how far we are prepared to trust one another. I think it's worth taking the risk, and maintaining a watch. One of us sleeps two hours while the other stays awake and listens for anything that may be going on. If nothing happens, all well and good. If someone moves, wake up the other one, and we'll see what's going on.'

They were still surveying one another, trying to weigh up the odds. Denis said:

'Obviously we've got to take a chance. I'm all for the watch idea.'

The tension between them relaxed a little. Perhaps this return to a system they both knew so well eased their minds. Or perhaps one of them . . .

'No,' said Denis forcefully, 'I'm damned if I'll keep on thinking unpleasant thoughts. The two of us are sane and we're all here — no bits missing. I thought I was finished with watches and guard mounting, but it looks as though old habits die hard.'

'Who's first?' asked Frank.

Denis extended his palm, with a penny in it.

'Have a look that there aren't two

heads,' he invited.

'No, I think I can — '

'Have a look,' Denis insisted. 'I don't want to have you sitting there brooding while I'm asleep — or lying awake while I'm on watch.'

They both laughed. The coin spun. Frank said: 'Heads.' It was tails. Frank got into bed after removing his shoes and loosening his collar. His eyes were getting heavier, but he was surprised to find that otherwise he was not sleepy. He felt mentally alert, and even when he was slowly succumbing to the advance of drowsiness he knew that it would not be a deep, embracing slumber; he would be able to wake at once when the time came. 'Don't forget,' he muttered to the shape sitting on the end of the bed. 'Give me a shove as soon as anything moves. If anything happens, I want to *see* it happening. I don't like things going on unless I'm fully conscious.'

'Get your head down and stop nattering,' said Denis. 'I won't forget you.'

★ ★ ★

Nora unwillingly pulled back the curtain, driven by a nagging compulsion that she could not resist.

The sight that met her eyes was almost a disappointment. She had been prepared for horror — she had been drawn to it — but the jagged ruins were in no way terrifying. At least, not at first sight . . .

She realised that their apparent stillness was deceptive. The faint red glow that clung to the walls like some shining fungus ebbed and flowed, surging up and then down again so that the ceiling of her room was bathed in rhythmic flushes of unhealthy colour. That was all there was to be seen. But as she continued to look, she sensed a movement behind the walls, in the centre where the arch stood. There was a ghostly palpitation, a movement like slow, exultant dancing. This was a night of rejoicing on the other side. 'The other side' — she could not repress a shudder. What else could one call it?

She let the curtain slip back into place. This was all too fantastic to be thought over carefully. Even now she had only the vaguest idea of the danger with which they were threatened. She wished that it had been possible to have a long talk with Simon, so that she would know what to expect in the morning. This alternating swing of farce and terror left no clear impression on the mind. She recalled the horror of that strange world into which she and Frank had wandered, and knew that they had been afraid, but she could not say what had caused that fear. The shapes and the furtive movements were indistinct now. She could not recollect — and she certainly could not fit them into any clear conception of what the world would be like after tomorrow. This was a world of science and normality. Trains and black magic ... electricity and witchcraft ... power houses and blood-stained altars ... ? These things were mutually exclusive. It was foolish to believe that a chanting of spells before a heap of ruins could loose the hordes of prehistoric terror on a world that had outgrown such superstition. Impossible ... but for the inescapable conviction of evil crouching outside the house, waiting for the morning. And to fight it, only Simon?

I could do with a drink of water, she thought. Supper would have been a mockery, but a drink would have been welcome. A drink of water. The mere thought began to torment her. And if she went down for a drink, she might have a word with Simon. That was really what she needed: she did not believe that Simon, knowing as much as he obviously did, would succumb to Jonathan's influence. Whoever was possessed by that venomous little creature, it was not Simon.

In which case, it was somebody else . . .

Here she was facing the problem again, finding reasons for dismissing the possibility that anyone in the house could be the powerless creature who was to be the source of life energy for the returning gods.

There was no sound from the next room. Denis and Frank were silent. The oppression of death weighed on her; it was not only the cold that made her shiver. The need to talk to someone became imperative.

* * *

Mrs. Morris breathed heavily, at intervals breaking into a slight, spluttering snore. Her husband lay with his eyes open and looked steadfastly at the ceiling. Once he moved, and Mrs. Morris stirred uneasily in her sleep. 'Mm?' she said from a great distance.

He made no reply.

* * *

Denis shook Frank. Frank's eyes opened reluctantly and he opened his mouth to speak, but Denis put his hand quickly across it.

'Someone's just walked past the door,' he said.

Frank blinked to signify that he was awake and had understood. He swung out of bed, and the two of them went cautiously across to the door.

12

Nora hesitated at the top of the stairs. The candle illuminated only a few steps, the remainder plunging away into abysmal gloom. She almost turned back.

Afraid of compromising yourself, Nora fach? The idea was laughable. On a night like this, ordinary considerations were swept aside by the necessity of combating her loneliness: it was essential that she should go down and talk to Simon. Until she had a chance of sorting out the muddle in her mind and of finding out what their chances were of resisting the onslaught of these malign forces stamping eagerly at the gateway, she could not possibly rest. Each moment had become more nerve-racking. Lying in bed, she had remembered a story, read long ago, about a room in which the ceiling came down — or was it the canopy of one of those old-fashioned four-poster beds? — to crush the occupant. She was trembling, falling in and then agitatedly scrambling out of that morass of half-sleep which is haunted by indefinable shapes, where every thought is swiftly translated into dream images, elusive but terrifying. The sound of another human voice . . . the thought of it was like the pangs of a thirst that must be quenched.

Nora drew her dressing-gown tighter and went downstairs. There was a faint crack of light under the door at the end of the passage. As she approached, the door opened and Simon stood there, peering towards her. He was still fully dressed, and as he stood aside to let her enter, she saw that the blankets on the couch had not been disturbed.

'What's the matter?' asked Simon in a low voice.

She closed the door, and replied in the same tone. 'Jonathan sleeps in the room above; we mustn't let the sound of our voices wake him up.'

'He won't wake: for him this is a night of rest and preparation. His psychic energies need to be conserved, ready for their great trial tomorrow — or is it today?' He glanced at the inaccurate clock.

'Couldn't we go up and overpower him? We could wake Frank and Denis — '

'Jonathan may be sleeping, but he's by no means unprotected.' Simon sat on the edge of the couch and indicated that she should sit beside him. 'Now, then — what brought you down here at this hour?'

Because the kitchen was warm and safe, she found that the things she had come to ask sounded foolish. She said: 'Why aren't you getting some rest yourself, ready for the morning?'

'Don't change the subject. Did you come down to see me about something?'

There was an unfathomable look in his eyes. Behind the studious, remote Simon that she knew was somebody else, looking out at her through his eyes. This fleeting awareness, pricking at so many ready suspicions in her mind, made her move instinctively a few inches away.

'What is it?' Simon demanded.

He was turned towards her, and unexpectedly he put his hand on her arm. It was warm and compelling; she sensed

238

an emotion that he had never shown before.

'Nora . . . when this is over, and we can talk reasonably — '

'But how is it going to finish?' she asked hurriedly, alarmed by his manner, and seizing the opportunity his words offered to bring up the subject that had brought her down here. 'Do you know how it will all end — and if you do, couldn't you tell us? I can't get to sleep; I want to know what we've got to face in the morning. If you have any power to fight all these horrible things . . . I mean, if you know, Simon, why can't you say what's going to happen?'

'Nothing's certain,' said Simon evasively.

'You might fail?'

'Fail?'

He savoured the word as though it was one that had never before occurred to him. 'Fail . . . ' But he did not answer, and she thought that he smiled. His hand still lay on her arm, and he was studying her face with a disturbing, keen appraisal that was new to her. She said: 'Simon, please let's have an end to this mystery.'

'I've been too much occupied lately,' he said, musing, 'but soon it will all be over, and then things will be very different.'

She freed herself from his grasp.

'What chance have we,' she said slowly and deliberately, 'of assistance from the White Adepts?'

It was the first thing she had said that really seemed to reach him. His eyes narrowed. 'We don't know that they exist,' he said. 'What are they now? They were never a clique, as the Black Adepts were. When their work was over, what did they become? Their appearances when it seemed necessary to strike another blow at the powers of sorcery — who has ever explained them? They could hardly be called appearances: rather, a display of power, a sort of pyrotechnical exhibition. And how do we know what their characteristics may be today? It is my belief that the White Adepts are no longer a body of men; if they exist at all, it is as a spiritual force — an incredibly refined force, perhaps attenuated so much' — his lip curled — 'that it now possesses no physical strength whatever. Evil becomes more and more active, and takes on more and more body as it flourishes; but the aim of all purer philosophies is non-existence, a bodiless Nirvana, a state where all but contemplation is forbidden. The White Adepts . . . I think they've been translated to another plane, where meditation alone is of value, and where no storms are permitted to disturb their ivory towers. Evil is an active force; good is passive.'

There was in his voice none of the comfort that Nora was seeking. That strangely mocking pessimism disturbed her. She said:

'Simon — are you the one Jonathan chose last night?'

'Would I tell you if I were?'

Again she was rebuffed. Abruptly she rose, wanting to get away. He stood beside her.

'You're not what we'd hoped — one of the White Adepts?' she asked, inviting the final disillusionment.

'I am not.'

Until he spoke, she had not realised

how much she had been clinging to the comforting belief.

'And the help we need . . . ? Tomorrow, when Jonathan starts — '

He took her by the shoulders, and again there was an unknown Simon looking out at her.

'Asceticism isn't everything,' he burst out fiercely. 'It's been a long, hard struggle, but the time's at hand when the training and the suffocating of all natural impulses will be at an end. Because I've been so deeply involved in books and the old lore for so long, don't think I've been blind to you, Nora.'

'Simon — '

'If it will put your mind at rest' — his eyes were shining — 'I'll tell you now what will happen in the morning. You shall hear it all. You may not sleep . . . but at least there'll be enough splendid thoughts and dreams to make lying awake a pleasure.' He laughed, then stood absolutely still. 'What was that?'

Distinctly they heard the long rasping of a loose board on the landing at the head of the stairs. Simon was at once withdrawn into a world of his own, from which he emerged at last with an enigmatic sigh. 'Your brother,' he said decisively.

'How do you know?'

'It was your brother, with his friend,' Simon said.

Nora opened the door and heard a slight scuffling noise.

'Everyone's on the prowl,' said Simon ironically. She could tell at once that his excitement had died down, and that he would probably not tell her what had been on the tip of his tongue a moment ago.

She was right. He said: 'You'd better go back to bed, or even in times of stress like these we'll have a lot of gossip on top of our other troubles.' The thought seemed to amuse him.

Now, as she found herself walking automatically out into the passage, she had a dozen questions she wanted to ask.

'Simon, what happened to Frank and myself in the castle the other day? How was it that we could walk through into that world, and yet you say the creatures in there can't get out until some sort of ritual has been gone through? We got in and out: why — '

'Until the Great Seal has been broken, no-one may come out. The gateway is open, but there is no way through from the other side. Jonathan performed the ceremony that opened it, and then left it for the cosmic upheaval to settle down: around that arch is a state of terrific flux, through which you, by a freak of nature, were able to walk. The whole corner of the cosmos was stable for a short period, and you got in — and, by a stroke of luck, got out again, when you might well have been trapped. It's hard to explain, but you were not physically in that world: it was only that the forces in that area were so strong that you saw it exactly as it is, your mind completely controlled by the reflection of the distant universe in which the old gods lie waiting. That doesn't mean there was no danger — you might easily have succumbed to the powers of that world, and been consumed . . . bodily, or spiritually — I don't really know. But I do know that, despite the fact that you could apparently go into that other world, none of the inhabitants can come out until the word is given. It's always easier,' he added grimly, 'for one in a state of grace to fall from it into hell than for one of the denizens of hell to climb up into the light.'

'If Jonathan could be prevented from breaking the seal — '

'More than that would be necessary to make the world absolutely safe. By making the preliminary moves, Jonathan has put the equilibrium of the whole creation in a perilous state. The gate must be wholly opened or wholly closed: it cannot be left as it is. Now run along, and put everything out of your mind until the dawn. I'll do the worrying.'

So far from being reassured by their conversation, Nora had been profoundly unsettled. Nothing definite had been explained, and she was left with an intense dissatisfaction; she was chilled and miserable as she went back upstairs, not unaware of the quiet closing of one of the doors on the landing. She was on the verge of going straight into her brother's room to challenge him, but weariness, darkness and bewilderment weighed her down. It would only involve long explanations on her part. Besides, she had only Simon's word for it that the noise had been caused by Denis. Why should Denis have been trying to spy on her? . . . unless he was Jonathan's chosen instrument . . . The insoluble problem was posed again, adding itself to her irritation over Simon's unsatisfactory replies.

Again she pulled the curtain back from the window. The snow rose towards the castle, focal point of all the evil that had been banished from the world in the dark past. On the other side of the house it would be falling in a long, white road to the village below — the village that was so near yet so unattainable.

Nora began to wonder, not very optimistically, whether that barrier was still surrounding the house. There was no reason to suppose that Jonathan would have relaxed his precautions. But even if the barrier were still there, wouldn't it be better to leave the house and hide somewhere, on the off-chance of being able, during the confusion — for she could visualise the morning only as hideous confusion — to slip away and give warning?

Warning — to whom?

And what could be done against these things, shapes, forces, disembodied spirits of evil . . . ? Nora was overcome by a sudden comprehension of the essential weakness of man, his puny strength, and his utter helplessness in the face of pure evil.

She heard what might have been the voices of Frank and Denis talking, and was glad that others were as sleepless as she was.

★ ★ ★

'What do you suppose she was doing?' said Denis.

Frank shook his head moodily. 'How should I know? She's your sister — I don't know what she's like.'

'Don't be an idiot — she's not as fond of Simon as all that.'

'I thought at first. .' Frank left the sentence unfinished, but Denis looked up in comprehension.

'Thought she was Jonathan's little servant going to prepare for the great moment?' he said.

'We still have no proof she's not.'

'We've no proof of anything,' said Denis. 'We're all nuts. Two and two make five. All this is beyond me. I can't get the hang of it at all; I can't explain — '

'Talking of explaining,' Frank interrupted in a low voice, 'how are we to explain Brennan's body, lying there stretched out in your front room?'

'Who do you want to explain to?'

'Police — after this is all over.'

'Police? Village constables don't fit into this at all. Unless things take a turn for the better, old son, we won't need to explain anything to anybody — it'll all be out of our hands. And if it does work out all right . . . mm, it would be hard, wouldn't it? A black magic story wouldn't go down very well.'

'They'd hardly believe it.'

'I'm not sure that I believe it myself,'

said Denis. 'It's just outside my comprehension altogether. After you've thought about it long enough, it ceases to be frightful and becomes downright silly.'

Frank said: 'If you'd seen what Nora and I saw when we went under that arch . . . '

Denis looked at the watch lying on the chest of drawers. 'Your turn, brother.' He rolled into bed and lay awake, while Frank settled on the end of the bed and drew a blanket about his shoulders.

'Have you thought about making a dash for it?' asked Denis.

'When — in the morning?'

'Any time. Cut and run for it. Even if we couldn't get past that little screen our devilish friend has put around the house, we might hide somewhere and perhaps make a nuisance of ourselves.'

'It's a long chance.'

'Sure, it's a long chance. If Jonathan is as bright as he seems to be, he could probably find us and fetch us back: any sorcerer would be able to cook up a spell that would root us out and bring us running. But it would upset him — put him off his stroke. I have an idea that friend Jonathan doesn't like to exert himself — '

'Wastes his psychic energy, doing that sort of thing,' said Frank thoughtfully, as though the words did not mean very much to him.

'Exactly.'

It was too dark for either of them to see the other's face. Frank said carefully: 'We're assuming that neither of us has any prior engagement with Jonathan.'

'That's something we've got to assume: we're agreed on that.'

'Run for it . . . And leave your sister — and your mother and father — to face the music?'

Denis was silent.

'I don't see how we can go,' Frank went on, 'unless we all go. Common sense says get going, and leave the others: it won't do any good for us all to stick here. But you can't do it, can you?'

'And we can't take the others,' said Denis, 'because each extra one is an extra chance of having Jonathan's chosen one with us. All right, then — that's out.' He turned over and punched his pillow. 'The time's going damned slowly.'

Neither of them voiced the opinion that this cold vigil throughout the night was futile: the two hours of the watch went more slowly than any that they had known during the war, but they would not give up. If there had been any distrust earlier, it was gone now.

'If you're not the same Frank I knew,' said Denis, 'you're wasting a lot of time putting up a show.'

'I was thinking the same about you,' came the reply.

They shivered in the bitter air, and Frank looked at the time.

'Not long,' he said.

'What are we expecting?'

'I've no idea.'

It was during Denis's watch, shortly before he was due to awaken Frank, that the sound of footsteps was again audible along the landing outside. Denis shook his colleague, and they sat still for a moment. The footsteps passed their door. Frank was pulling his shoes on as Denis opened the door cautiously.

'Who is it?'

'Jonathan.'

Frank stood up. 'This is it.'

'Must be going down to make his preparations — '

'And to get Simon.'

'You think that Simon — ?'

'I've felt it all along.'

Jonathan stopped at the head of the stairs. He had been moving stiffly, as though recently awakened from a dream or a reverie so deep that he was unable to adjust himself to the waking world. He stopped and turned, but it was as though something pulled at him, insisting that he should continue on his way.

Denis whispered: 'He's still drowsy. He's probably been keeping some sort of meditative silence during the night, like they're supposed to, and he's not fully conscious. Let's rush him.'

'Don't be a fool. He's certain to be — '

'It's worth it. He's a dangerous animal, but he's sleepy. Quickly — before we lose the chance.'

Frank did not hesitate any longer. He and Denis moved out swiftly into the open, in the faint light that seeped in through the landing window. Jonathan wavered: he was like a man trying to focus on something too elusive for him. The two men flung themselves forward, Denis going for his throat and Frank catching him about the body. They were prepared for almost any dreadful shock, but Jonathan offered no resistance. He uttered a sharp cry, and sank beneath their weight. His head met the floor with a thud, and he lay still.

Denis sat back, puzzled. 'That's queer . . . I thought we might get him unawares, but I didn't expect anything like this.'

Frank said: 'If he comes round again, we may not be so lucky. What can we do?'

Downstairs, a door grated open.

'What's that? What's going on up there?' It was Simon, his voice sharp and full of alarm. For some reason, they remained silent, and then there was the sputter of a match, and Simon came upstairs.

Nora's door opened slightly. She left it ajar and stood away from the opening, looking out at the group crouched in shadow at the head of the stairs.

'I'll get a candle,' said Frank.

Simon reached the top and gave an angry exclamation as his match went out. Nora wondered whether the failure of the match was responsible for this cry, or whether it was something to do with the huddled shape of Jonathan. If Simon had been in Jonathan's power, perhaps this new turn of events — she had heard the brief scuffle, and could now guess what had happened — had freed him.

Light flared up again, and Frank put his candle on the banister. Wax dripping on to the rail, make a mess, have to clean it up, thought Nora absurdly. She wished she could see Simon's face.

He said tersely: 'You fools.'

'What do you mean by that?' Frank demanded.

'Don't you know what risks you're running?'

'We figured we'd get nowhere without taking some risks,' said Denis contemptuously, 'instead of sitting back and letting trouble come looking for us.'

'Very brave, I'm sure. But physical

violence won't work in matters like this — '

'It's worked,' said Denis.

'Temporarily. You've taken Jonathan unawares. When he recovers, what do you suppose will happen?'

'We'd better tie him up,' said Denis, turning as though to return to his room.

He was halted. Nora saw his movements slow down, like a film that is running down, and he swung one unavailing arm with infinite heaviness in the air. A fly struggling in treacle . . .

Jonathan sat up.

'Foolish,' he said. 'Very foolish. I don't like my arrangements to be upset. You'll pay for this — both of you.'

He excluded Simon, Nora realised. She took a step further away from the door, filled with a tingling horror of his looking in her direction and seeing into the darkness of the room.

Simon said: 'Rash people. They should have left their fate in my hands, shouldn't they, Mr. Jonathan?'

Jonathan's voice was expressionless as he replied. 'It might have been better for them. Striking me . . . no, that was a silly thing.'

Denis and Frank were still held, swaying and writhing in slow convulsions, their whole appearance so unnatural that Nora put her hand to her mouth and tried to stifle the harsh noise that choked in her throat. She could not look away. She saw Jonathan hunched against the wall, watching, and then Simon lifted his hand, and Frank and Denis were free — free to stagger against the wall beside Jonathan.

'Thanks,' gasped Denis, 'but why didn't you do that right away? If you can just arrange for something like that to fix Jonathan himself — and don't unlock him in the way you've just done us — we'll see that he doesn't cause any mischief. When the dawn breaks, Mr. Jonathan will be fastened up as securely as my cash box used to be.'

'What makes you think I could do it?' asked Simon.

'Well . . . '

Denis looked from Simon to Jonathan. Nora saw him shrug, and she saw

Jonathan's seamed, bitter face.

'If you don't want another dose — '

'All right,' said Frank wearily, 'we'll go back to bed like good little boys.'

'Oh, no,' said Jonathan. 'I think perhaps you should all come downstairs so that you can be . . . together. It's nearly time. I was about to make my arrangements.'

Nora put her hand on the window-ledge and propped herself against it.

Jonathan said: 'Would you be good enough to wake the others, so that we can proceed? Nice to have you all in one place. I want no interference. If you can't be trusted to lie still in bed, you'd better assemble downstairs. No interference at all: take that as a warning, if you please.'

He gestured along the landing. Denis reluctantly came towards Nora's door. She pushed the window up, trembling in case it should squeak, and looked out at the fleecy snow rising below her.

★   ★   ★

Denis said: 'I can't help it: she's just not there.'

257

'How long . . . ?'

'How the hell should I know?'

Jonathan seized the candle and went into Nora's room. Mr. and Mrs. Morris came out of their room and stood with the others. Mrs. Morris drew a coat about her, shivering; but her mouth was set and defiant.

Simon said quietly: 'That's very silly of her. She can't get far.'

'Catch her death, she will,' said Mrs. Morris.

'It won't do any good at all,' said Simon. 'I think we ought to fetch her back.'

Denis said: 'Good luck to her.'

'It won't be good luck for anyone who's caught out in the open this dawning. I'll go and look for her.'

Mr. Morris, coughing and catching at his chest, left his wife's side. 'I know the place, Simon, man; I'll go. Bad it is for her to be out in this. I'll go.'

Simon shook his head. 'I'm the one to fetch her,' he said decisively.

13

The snow, looking so safe and receptive from the window, had been deep. Nora was wet. If I had only thought of getting away earlier, and got dressed . . . She hugged the coat about her as the cold wind struck at her, and could almost have gone back into the house. The wall of the barn gave some protection. If only her father had not been so conscientious in locking up the stable, she might have hidden in there for some time, but ever since they bought the new trap he had been ridiculously careful. Inside the barn would be better than this. She walked around it, her teeth chattering as she turned the corner. Or perhaps the old shed by the hen-house; but that was small and bare, and anyone who came searching for her would only have to open the door to find her.

The thought of Jonathan coming after her was a spur. There were no lights now from the village, but she could feel its comfortable presence down the slope, and longed to make a dash for it. Wet, chilled, miserable — it would still be worth it if she thought she could get there. But it was so unlikely.

Nora went into the barn. In summer, years ago, it had been a wonderful place. You could hide in the barn, and even people who knew you were in there had a job to find you. Now it seemed huge, cold, and unprotective. There was nothing that a torch could not seek out. She wondered whether Jonathan had a torch. And whether she could not manage to run for it even if Jonathan did come to find her. It might take him a minute or two to locate her, and perhaps she could slip out.

It wasn't worth it. It would have been better to stay in the house with the others. Whatever was coming could best be faced in the company of others. If she had not succumbed to that burst of panic, that sudden surging will to self-preservation . . . But she would not go back now. Having made such a move, nothing would drive her into the house again.

Until someone came for her.

Waiting for someone to come — as she was sure he would — she was, in one inexplicable moment that had all the quality of a mystical revelation, convinced of the menace that hung over the world. It had not been real before. It was not until she crouched in the shadows that she knew how real it all was. There was no reason why it should be now more than any other time: she was cold and wretched, more like a little girl who wants to get home to a warm fire and affectionate care, but her mind was clearer than it had been all day. Almost calmly, she understood that this was a crucial moment in the history of mankind and all the great spiritual forces that had gone to the making of mankind; she would not, could not possibly have been here, cowering like a hunted animal, if the natural order of things had not been cruelly upset. This was a feeble gesture of defiance — a frightened, purposeless defiance — but it was the gesture of humanity against the powers of darkness. Human stubbornness and some deeper, indefinable instinct kept her here. Nuisance value, she thought, knowing the phrase to be appropriate, though she had no idea where she could have picked it up.

There was the sound of feet crunching in snow. She had been expecting it. The barn seemed to contract, so that she was pinned in her corner, with no way out. Whoever came in would fill the place: there would be no way round, no path to the door, no escape. With a salt taste in her mouth, she crouched in bitter resignation as the threatening noise came closer.

There was no respite. He did not explore the other outhouses first. He came straight to the barn, and she saw the faint oblong of the door filled with his dark outline. He said:

'Nora.'

Surprise at hearing Simon's voice almost tempted her to answer, but the taut self-control that had prevented her from returning to the house refused to let her speak. She waited, sure that the sound of her breathing and unavoidable shudders could be heard from a considerable distance away.

'Nora,' said Simon again. Then he came into the barn.

His shadow was lost in other shadows. Only the sound of his quiet, untroubled movements came to her ears. She could tell that he was walking across the floor towards her, and there was a cat-like confidence in his walk that assured her it would be useless to run. He could see her; he knew where she was.

He came right up to her and stood beside her, though even now she could not be sure that the dark shape was not just another of the black smudges that made a regular procession before her eyes in this enveloping gloom.

'You'll be cold, Nora,' he said.

'I'm all right.'

'You shouldn't be out here like this. Come back to the house, Nora; everyone's up, and they're all worried about you.'

She said: 'You don't sound particularly worried.'

'I had no difficulty in telling where you were. I came straight to you.'

She throbbed with the fear that he would reach out and touch her; the anticipation set her nerves on edge. But he stood motionless.

'I feel safer out here,' she said.

'You're being silly,' he said. 'Inside, it's warm.'

'I'll stay here. Who sent you?'

'I came of my own accord.'

'That's nice of you, Simon,' she said flatly. 'You'd better go back and tell them you can't find me.'

He said, unexpectedly: 'That's what I intend doing.'

'Then why — '

'Are you cold, Nora?'

She could tell, without seeing, that he had made some small movement, and at once she felt an unaccountable warmth stealing through her. 'That's a useful accomplishment,' she said, with a shaky laugh.

'I have many more,' he said dryly. 'The time is coming when you shall see them. I insisted on coming out to look for you because I wanted to make sure that you would stay here. I should have been disappointed if I had been able to persuade you to return to the house: I like your independence; you show that you do not consider yourself bound to the family — that really you feel an urge to get away from them and fight your own fights, as it were.'

She derived no pleasure from this uncanny warmth that he had produced. What he was saying was wild and irrational. She said:

'What are you talking about? I shouldn't have deserted the rest of them, but I felt that I couldn't stay in the house any longer. I thought . . . well, I'm not at all sure now. If you think I ought to go back and stick with the others — '

'No, that's just what you mustn't do. You're meant to strike out on your own, to be unconventional. The fetters of this cramped, degenerate world — '

'Keep away,' cried Nora abruptly, then relaxed. It had been a false alarm.

'I'm not going to touch you,' said Simon gently. 'Until afterwards, I need all my strength, and it is fatal for an adept to indulge in sensual pleasures before a great ritual. Many have failed in times past because of that: the incantations that followed sensual orgies were doomed to failure.'

'An adept?' Nora echoed. 'But you said — '

'Will you promise to stay here if I tell you the truth? I don't want to keep you here against your will — I shall have to draw reserves of energy from Jonathan in order to enclose your family — so it would be of the greatest assistance if you could wait here during the great consummation . . . wait until I come for you.'

It was all disjointed; the pieces did not fit together. Nora wondered whether Simon had stepped over the borderline into the world of insanity — or whether this was all a part of Jonathan's plan, directed towards some end that she could not conceive. And simultaneously other more horrible ideas were forming in her mind as she tried to find some coherence in Simon's ravings.

'Afterwards,' he said, 'when we can say

that the task is well done, and then sit back in our new world, strong once more in the glory of the community of adepts — '

'Simon. Tell me what you're talking about.'

He gave vent to a deep, satisfied chuckle. 'Even you have been deceived. I was afraid that you — who I thought might have been close to me in spirit, and therefore able to detect things more easily — might have seen from the start what was in preparation. Will you stay here until it is all finished, and then join me? For in the courts of the dark gods there is no aesceticism, and the wearisome struggle with books and the documents of the Atlantean priests will be at an end. After victory, there is relaxation.'

'You're Jonathan's slave,' she accused him.

'No. Jonathan is mine.'

His exultance was like a leaping warmth. She was still afraid that in this new, mad mood he would try to take hold of her. 'Simon — '

'It's warm here,' he said in a coaxing

voice. 'Stay here, where it's safe — '

'Safe? What about my mother and father, and Denis, and Frank?'

'They will not leave the house.'

Speech has no meaning when the words are uttered by a madman. Nora, groping, said: 'You mean they won't come out into the open until it's all over?'

'They mean nothing to you,' said Simon unemotionally. 'Be honest: we — you and I, Nora — are of a different breed. They are weak, and they will not be missed. There will be millions more like them, useless. They will not leave the house: they will never leave.'

She said weakly: 'During that seance, or whatever you choose to call it — '

'Why don't you sit down? There is no need to fear the cold or the damp. There is no discomfort from now on. We are the rulers of the universe; the elements are our servants.'

She was lapped in seductive warmth, somehow sitting down, comfortable and almost acquiescent, but with something inside her that would not break before this insidious attack.

'Let me explain briefly,' Simon went on, 'so that you will not be frightened when I leave you here alone for a short time. During what you call our little seance, I took possession of Jonathan: Jonathan is the one who is possessed, ready to play his part — not, I may say, the part he anticipated — in the recall of the gods. He knew from the start that I was to be feared, but he could not tell how much I knew. He feared me as a possible White Adept, and he knew that his own powers were not as strong as they ought to be: he believed himself a descendant of the Atlantean priests, but he was puzzled by his lack of real power. It was lust for domination that drove him on. He took the risk of being destroyed because he saw the possibility of a world in which he would be one of the chosen ones. And all the time he was playing into my hands. *I* am Simon, son of the Black Adepts. Fully conscious, as Jonathan could never have been, of the great responsibilities and the task that lay before me, I have spent my life seeking the books that hold the secret of the great rebirth, and while still a young man I have been fortunate enough to reach the end of this long quest that has covered so many centuries. Jonathan was a dabbler, an amateur magician, a product of spiritualist societies and psychic quacks — a man with some talents but no tradition, nothing to give him the right to summon the ancient lords back to their domain. I was afraid of his coming because I felt he might do great harm. I felt that the time had not yet come for the opening of the gateway; we could not afford to have any mistakes and hideous catastrophes. But then I began to hope that all would be well. I heard the singing beyond the gate, and I knew that this must be an auspicious time. Jonathan was the man — puny, stupid little tool of fate — who had found the missing books that made your father's library complete. The missing pieces that I had despaired of seeing in my short lifetime were supplied. I let Jonathan carry out the preliminary rites. He opened the gateway, shut the area off from outside interference — and might then have gone ahead and been swallowed up in his own bungling magic, for he had no power to break the Great Seal; unfortunately his assistant, another foolish dabbler from a circle of spurious occultists, was accidentally killed. When I arrived next morning, I knew it was not merely a matter of breaking the seal or of attempting to close the gateway, as I had originally anticipated.'

Nora said in a choked whisper: 'You knew all along, when you were warning us that Jonathan must not come, that this was going to happen . . . ?'

'I don't seem to have made myself clear,' said Simon patiently. 'I knew he was coming. I suspected, from information I was given in a state of trance, that he had a great deal of knowledge that, used on its own, would be harmful. As he was not an adept, I was certain that he could not break the Great Seal, but he might open the gateway — as, indeed, he did. I expected him to be swallowed up: the gods are impatient, and if there was any way of reaching the human and dragging him through into their world, they would do so. All I intended to do was to look at whatever books Jonathan had brought, and close the gateway again, releasing the strain on our universe and on our interwoven dimensions. The time for the return of the gods was, I thought, not yet. But until I came here and probed into Jonathan's mind, I had no idea how much he really knew. Finding him alive, I knew a different approach was necessary — but I could not have imagined that it would be possible to go ahead with the fulfilment of our greatest dreams. I took possession of Jonathan: he is not an ideal servant, but he has had a certain amount of training, and his mind is attuned, however reluctantly, to the reception of the gods. Jonathan is to be the sacrifice — for that's what it amounts to — and I am to be that favoured adept whose reward shall be power over the new world, through the temples of the great gods. All knowledge is now mine, and the blood of my ancestors sings thankfully in my veins.'

He drew a deep breath of satisfaction.

Nora struggled to throw off the lethargy that was creeping over her. She could not account for this soothing warmth and the feeling that she was sitting at her ease in a comfortable room, with someone talking to her from afar. Forcing the words out, she said:

'Why have you waited until now to tell me the truth? Were you afraid that you couldn't cope with everyone else?'

'Afraid? There isn't one of them could hope to stand up against me. If Jonathan, with a certain amount of experience in lesser magic, could not prevail, what chance would there be for an ordinary mortal? No, I was not worried about the opposition of your family: I merely wished to carry on my preparations without annoying interference. All my psychic powers will be needed this morning: I was unwilling to squander them on conflict. I admit I slipped when I allowed him to be taken unawares by your brother and his stupid friend, but it was a minor mistake, easily glossed over. Instead of having to exert myself in the repression of enemies, I have been able to move freely and to spend an undisturbed night — apart, of course, from your welcome visit.'

'If I'd known — '

'You know now,' said Simon. 'Do you trust me now? Do you understand what I've been working for, and what a wonderful life is opening up ahead of us? This is why I haven't been as attentive as I might have been, Nora — I know it's been hard for you to realise why I was neglecting you — but everything will soon be different. Will you wait here while I — '

'You're completely insane,' she cried, standing up so that she should not be lulled to sleep. 'If I'd known what part you intended to play in this ghastly business — '

'Nora,' he said reproachfully; 'you know this isn't your real self speaking. Forget the conventional responses, and speak with your heart. This means power for both of us . . . and perhaps,' his voice rose with excitement, 'perhaps immortality, if the gods are good to us.'

She realised that nothing she could say would make any impression on him.

'Can I trust you?' he said pleadingly.

She refused to answer.

The air became suddenly colder, as though he had spitefully withdrawn his boon. He said: 'It's disappointing to find how much of the old existence still lingers on. You'll have to learn, Nora. I'm disappointed; it's annoying that I should have to waste my energies sealing you in here, instead of being able to trust you.'

'You can let me go back to the house,' she said coldly.

'Oh, no . . . I don't think you understand. The house is set apart for — well, for a certain purpose. When the gods come through, their retainers will come with them — strange beings such as you saw when you wandered through the gateway, and other wild children of distorted worlds. They have been faithful, and they deserve their reward, crude and bestial as they may be. It is usual for the warriors of a conquering army to be allowed to loot and pillage . . . and feast. I shall imprison your family in the house and leave them to entertain our hungry friends.'

The absurdity of it rose in Nora's mind. She began to laugh hysterically, sobbing out appeals to Simon to go away so that she could wake up. Then her conviction that it was a dream faded, and still it all seemed grotesque and funny in its fantastic impossibility. Through her tears and spasmodic laughter she watched Simon's dark shape flitting to and fro before her, and heard him muttering — to whom? Not to her.

'Who are you talking to?' she asked.

At last he stood still, and his rustling movements subsided into the unholy hush of this wicked dawn.

'You will stay here,' he said flatly. 'Afterwards, when you have realised how the world has been changed, you will be glad to accept my protection.'

Fancy, she thought, a great high priest wanting *me*, when he'll be in a position to choose anyone he desires. What a compliment, Nora fach. What a world he could make for me. I don't believe it, don't believe it, he's pulling my leg, it doesn't fit in with those horrors beyond the castle ruins, this is crazy . . .

Then she realised that she was alone, and collapsed, her sobs dying away and her head clearing. Simon had gone. She must think.

Think.

She stumbled to her feet and walked unsteadily forward a few steps, to be brought up sharply by a force that pressed her backwards. She put out a hand, and felt it imprisoned by a mocking intangibility that somehow could not be penetrated. Simon had not been threatening idly: he had seen that she was not in a mood to accept his sinister assurances, and had been forced to expend his jealously conserved pyschic energies on keeping her a prisoner until he had completed the rite. Nuisance value, she thought, with the return of sanity. The weaker he is, the more hope for the world.

The world of jubilant spring and warm summers, of friendship and delight, of sunsets on red autumn ground . . . were all these things to be lost? Was there no appeal against this hideous future? Desperately, Nora wondered what prayers could be offered up, and what hope there was of that spiritual force which had once succoured the White Adepts spreading itself now over this threatened countryside, a protective armour against the spears of evil.

It was almost dawn.

* * *

'Where's Nora?' demanded Frank.

Jonathan, sitting impassively before the fire, shook his head unconcernedly.

'You sent your henchman out after her,' Denis accused him. 'What was the idea — what's going on out there?'

'I wouldn't advise you to try to go and see,' Jonathan said flatly.

Denis writhed impotently. 'If anything happens to her — '

'You'll shortly have other things to worry about.'

Mrs. Morris leaned forward in her chair. She had raked out the ashes and laid the fire. The first yellow flames flickered icily. The light of the oil lamp seemed less bright than it did in the evening, and failed to dispel the darkness that lingered in expectation of the dawn's more determined onslaught.

'I'll put the kettle on in a minute,' said Mrs. Morris.

Jonathan, after a moment, emitted a mirthless cackle. His responses were slow — almost, thought Frank, as though everything that he heard had to be transmitted somewhere else and a reply given before any sound could be uttered. It might be something to do with the state of concentration supposed to be necessary for all occult feats. Jonathan's remoteness would not prevent his acting viciously and compellingly if needs be.

Then they heard Simon coming back. He scraped his boots on the step, and the door swung open. He was alone.

Denis said: 'Where's Nora?'

'I couldn't find her.'

Frank started up. 'We'd better all have a look — '

'Sit down,' commanded Jonathan.

'We can't leave her out there, in the cold, while things are happening. She ought to be with us. We're going to look for her.'

As he spoke, Jonathan was backing

away. Simon made a complete circuit of the little group, twisting his hands together and talking under his breath like anyone who has just come in from the cold outside world and wishes to get warm again. Even so, there was something about his strangely mincing tread that aroused Frank's suspicions.

'What are you doing?'

Simon stopped his pacing, and stood away from them.

'Fastening you up all safe and sound,' he said complacently.

Jonathan walked around and stood beside him.

'It looks as though we were right,' said Denis; 'you're the one Jonathan took over. That's right, isn't it, Jonathan?'

Simon shook his head, smiling. 'As I've just been telling your sister — '

'Nora? But you just said — '

'As I've just been telling Nora,' Simon went on equably, 'you've all had it the wrong way round. I am in charge here: Jonathan is my servant. While you've been concentrating on our puny little friend here, I've been resting and taking what steps I considered necessary in preparation for the breaking of the Great Seal. I am the Black Adept who will open the gate wide. When the gods and their followers come through you will, alas, have only a short time left to live. But perhaps that is as well: as true lovers of what you call freedom, you would not welcome an existence of obedience and rigid control, would you?'

Denis and Frank, their faces pale with the anticipation of what they might meet, rose and tried to reach him, but found themselves penned in by that same force that had barred the way down to the village. Simon's contemptuous smile goaded them to a frenzied attempt to break through, but it was in vain.

'Where's Nora?' asked Denis.

'Perfectly safe; I didn't wish her to suffer the same fate as the rest of you.'

'You won't get away with this,' said Denis, all too well aware of his own futility.

'There's very little opposition that I can see.'

'Don't you feel that it's all too easy?'

said Frank in an affable tone. 'This isn't a struggle worth taking part in. All the dice are loaded. You have occult powers that place you far out of our class. There's no sport in it, no element of chance — no possible surprise. The game's all yours: is it worth playing that way? Wouldn't you like to give up your advantages just for a while and see how you get on in a straight fight?'

Simon laughed. 'A taunt like that isn't likely to draw me out.'

'I didn't think it would,' said Frank wryly.

'We've wasted enough time dealing with you people,' said Simon. 'The time has come. I'll say goodbye, then — and many thanks for your hospitality in the past, Mrs. Morris. I'm sorry I wasn't all you thought me.'

Mr. Morris, whose head had been sunk on his chest, looked up slowly.

'You're mistaken,' he said in a voice that was curiously unlike his normal way of speaking. 'Your aims have been quite clear. You have been watched for a long time. Watched . . . '

'By you?' said Simon, scornfully but uneasily.

'Not by me as a person.'

'What are you talking about, you old fool?'

Mr. Morris said: 'Who spoke of the White Adepts when you were taking possession of Jonathan? Whose voice was it that recounted the story of the Great Destruction? Not yours. There's an adversary waiting for you.'

Simon's face had paled. He took a step forward, then seemed to remember the existence of the barrier he had thrown around the group of people, and stopped. 'What makes you say that: what do you know about it?'

'I'm an old man,' said Mr. Morris. 'I know nothing about it. But even as an old man I am an instrument of divine good, as we all are. Men are the instruments of good and evil, and just as the voice of wickedness speaks through your mouth, so the voice of truth speaks through mine. Can you answer my question?'

Jonathan said: 'There's someone — something — behind him . . . beyond him . . . '

'Be quiet.'

'Why tell him to be quiet?' said Mr. Morris gently. 'He's your slave. He speaks only what you allow. Somewhere inside you is a thought that wills him to speak as he does. Do you, then, see someone behind and beyond this mortal frame?'

'No,' said Simon desperately. 'No. I see nothing. This is a trick. A vague threat — but I am not to be frightened. Nothing will stop me now.'

As he spoke, his eyes lit up, for the new expression of strange vitality had died from Mr. Morris's face, and he sank back into his usual slumped position, apparently losing all interest in the scene.

Simon gave a deep sigh. 'The White Adepts are too lazy to stir,' he said. 'I propose to leave you now. You need not fear that the period of waiting will be too agonisingly long. The psychic emanations of the circle I have drawn around you will attract the servants of the gods immediately. They will come and' — he bowed derisively — 'then it will soon be over.'

He turned to Jonathan, whose lack-lustre eyes were fixed on the far wall, seeing nothing.

'A worthy end to your fine scheme, my friend,' he said. 'You are to play your part, humble as it is, in the recall of the great masters. Shall we go?'

There was a wild exhilaration in his features, flushed as they had never been before. Denis had never seen Simon like this before: it was a completely different picture from the studious, pale young man who browsed — so innocuously, one would have thought — through those accursed books. For a moment resentment flared in Denis's mind against his father, who had stubbornly and foolishly kept those books. An old man's whim would be responsible for the destruction of civilisation. It was always the way — the whims of old men and unthinking fools had plunged the world into most of its wars and persecutions; and now the end of all that was most valuable and constructive in man's endeavours was at hand.

Simon, after one last comprehensive

look around the room, opened the door. There was the faintest suspicion of dull, steely light in the east. Jonathan walked behind Simon like a shadow.

They went out, and the door closed.

Nora sat with her head in her hands. Physical attempts to escape, and awkward, self-conscious, prayer had both proved useless. Whatever she tried to think of, and whatever hopes of a last-minute reprieve she might try to conjure up, only the vision of what she and Frank had seen in the ruined castle would come into clear focus. At any moment now the tension that existed between the two worlds might be broken, and those dreadful hordes would come pouring in. What would they be like on this earth? Great shapes or mere drifting clouds of abomination? It was impossible to conceive them as anything but grotesque animals, yet she knew they were something less physical, more terrifying than that. All normal conceptions would have to be warped in order to cope with the idea of these beings: no bounding, ludicrous monsters from story books, but predatory all-pervading forces from which there would be no escape, no concealment.

And Simon, most despicable of all creatures, willing to turn this abomination loose on humanity to satisfy his own perverted lust for power . . . More than anything, she dreaded Simon's triumphant, possessive return.

★   ★   ★

Denis was beginning to sob dryly with frustration. This captivity was tearing at his reason.

Frank said: 'There's nothing we can do. Nothing anyone could do. Maybe we ought to sing . . . or something.' He laughed awkwardly, mirthlessly.

'It may be,' said Mr. Morris slowly, speaking with his own voice and yet fumbling, as though trying to sort out a confusion of thoughts and strange disturbances at the back of his mind, 'that this is part of a great plan . . . a mighty trap. It may be.'

14

Simon and Jonathan climbed the hill towards the castle. The packed snow rasped under their feet, beginning to sparkle with the early light. From the castle came a faint, pulsating intimation of another subdued light, shining through like a guiding beacon from another world. Simon fingered the knife in his pocket and began to mutter an invocation under his breath. A flaring exaltation beat out from the world beyond, and yet outside the turbulent ruins was absolute stillness — a snowy, reverent hush.

As Simon and his powerless companion approached the black huddle on the summit of the slope, there was a mighty stirring and heaving from within — a great pressure on the other side of the gateway.

The two men, one full of the confidence of his own unnatural powers, the other walking mechanically and unconscious of what lay ahead, were almost under the shadow of the outer walls, crooked above them like scarred talons, when the voiceless clamour from inside was answered by a restless movement that throbbed through the air and the ground as though set up by a distant earth tremor. Simon came to a halt. Not only from inside the ruins, but from all around, came the psychic vibrations — vibrations that were hostile to himself and to all that he stood for. Drowning out the urgent welcome that had been coming like a clarion call through the archway, came the persistent throbbing of some mighty defiance, a surging, threatening storm. And the sense of someone watching him from behind suddenly grew upon him and swung him round in his tracks.

Light streamed from the open door of the farmhouse — the door that he had quite definitely closed. Walking up towards him was the figure of a man he had left imprisoned within the unbreakable circle. Mr. Morris, upright, moving as a young man moves, came proudly up the slope with complete confidence.

'Quickly — it must be done quickly.'

Simon drew the knife from his pocket and seized Jonathan.

'Stop!'

It was Mr. Morris, but only the known shape of Mr. Morris: the command was issued with all the authority of the forces that were ranged behind him. This was not an old man who spoke, but a human husk used as a mouthpiece by a disincarnate spirit, asserting its dominion over the forces of black rebellion. Simon, shaken by the majesty of that voice, hesitated, but did not let go of the limp, unresisting Jonathan.

'Who speaks?'

Behind Morris came the others who had been imprisoned within the house, and from the direction of the barn Nora moved into the light. The dawn was sending out fine silver fingers of benediction over the earth.

'I speak with the voice of that Being of wisdom and beauty into whose essence flowed the spirits of the White Adepts many centuries ago. Thus translated, these spiritual forces that once activated the bodies of truth-seeking men have been withdrawn from the world, but not oblivious to the sufferings of the world. They have been plunged in the deepest meditation, but whenever they have been called on, in times of great stress or in the accents of the humblest prayer, they have allowed their light to shine on the earth. Their sleep has been the sleep of spiritual refreshment and knowledge, but their watchfulness has never slackened. Evil disturbances send out emanations of wickedness that stir the adepts when the time comes. No great concentration of forces such as this could escape their notice.'

Nora reached out unsteadily, and Frank's arm was there to support her. She watched her father, his figure erect and strangely unknown to her, standing at the foot of the slope. She watched him moving up towards the two men up by the ruins, suddenly puny and frightened. His tone of authority rang like a massive bell in the frosty air.

Simon's voice drifted weakly down, its arrogance gone.

'It's too late to try threatening. You should have pitted yourself against me before — you would have understood then how futile your attempts would be. I've read the books, and I know the prophecies.' He cried out something unintelligible, and behind him the shadowy outline of the great castle was momentarily sketched on the air; the sky was torn by a streak of flame. 'I am an adept,' called Simon, regaining some of his confidence. 'You cannot fight against the fulfilment of this destiny. I am a descendant of the Black Adepts, and all the world of spirits, forsaken ones and the legion of Annwn and worlds deeper than Annwn are at my call. You cannot harm me.'

An intense light began to glow around Mr. Morris. He went remorselessly on, and Simon seemed afraid to turn away. The uncannily straightened body of the old man was a blinding iridescence of power. He was a man who had awoken from no ordinary slumber: his whole deeper self had awoken, and he answered the frenzied jibes of the man above him with the voice of mankind and what was higher than mankind.

'I speak for all the souls who have ever

taken part in the conflict with evil since first life began to flourish in this cosmos. The books you sought have been waiting here a long time for your arrival. It was known that someone would come. When the families of the Black Adepts, defeated and scattered, lost track of many of their most precious volumes, they were assembled here to await the day when the most dangerous of adepts should come to seek them. If a city had been built over the ruins, the books would still have been preserved, and when the adept came to the archway, there would have been someone waiting. Waiting for him . . . This is a trap, high priest of evil: your Atlantean dreams are no more than dreams; you and your sacrificial lamb have brought us more of the accursed volumes to be consumed in this moment of destruction.'

Simon turned away by a great effort of will and bent down in the snow, his dark figure merging with the black shadows of the ruins. Nora's heart began to beat madly. If it should be too late to stop him . . .

The awful voice that spoke through her father went on, an even, undeterred voice that might have been addressing an erring friend in normal conversation, yet singing about the hills and valleys so that it was a wonder the whole countryside did not awaken. 'Cease your abominable incantations before it is too late, ignorant wretch. It is best that the solution of problems should be left to men alone. But when the scales are loaded too heavily, justice demands our intervention. Cease, before you call down everlasting wrath on yourself.'

An unspeakably repulsive, convulsive light was beginning to rise like a cloud of heavy smoke about Simon. Within the ruins the clamour rose to screaming heights, and the distance between the farmhouse and the castle seemed to contract, so that Nora, clutching Frank tightly, felt that she was standing on the very brink of that hideous world into which the two of them had once been plunged.

'It is a thing to be feared,' roared the voice of Morris, 'when the mantle of contemplation is cast off and the angels of light ride the skies.'

Nora closed her eyes. It made things no better. A thousand darting, smudged images chased across behind her eyelids, and the horror of what might be happening up in the ruins without her being conscious of it forced her eyes open again. Better to look, and know.

Denis said in a strained voice: 'If something doesn't break soon, our whole world will crack up: I can feel it.'

The grinding of two ships lying side by side in rough seas . . . the collision and shuddering of two worlds straining in an unnaturally warped space and time.

'Great God,' said Frank.

The ruins blazed into life. Against the glare that poured like liquid fire through the clearly defined arch, they saw Simon shrinking away, a cringing silhouette. The foulness of inhuman life bubbled in the archway, and a long ululating cry of triumph echoed down the valley. Simon stopped backing away, and they saw him hold out his arms in ecstatic welcome.

Frank said suddenly: 'Don't look.'

But there was no way of not looking

now. There was no way of hiding the eyes from those shapeless distortions of all that was right and natural — writhing through the gateway, spreading like uncontrolled slime into evil-coloured viscosity. A miasma of insupportable depravity . . . a stench of primeval fecundity . . . And advancing to meet it, like an inadequate David facing a giant whose magnitude knew no bounds, only that one small figure, radiating light. Yet he was, they suddenly realised, not alone. In the skies above was an unseen turbulence. Behind Morris as he walked up the slope was a powerful throbbing as of thousands of wings — a patient but menacing noise.

Simon turned to face him.

The gateway frothed evil. Colours changed and faded — colours never seen before on this earth, shining in from another world, another state of being. Simon, in a strong voice that spoke for all the wickedness surging out behind him, cried:

'Go back. You are too late. There will never be another Moytura: you have come too late.'

No human being, even the handful who were watching, would ever be able to give a clear account of what happened then. There are no terms in any human language that would adequately describe the clash that shook the hills around and brought forth the feeble answering cries of a hundred terrified dogs. Every living thing stirred and trembled.

What swooped from the air on the twisted beings that writhed through the gateway was formless and noiseless. It was not a cloud, but it fell upon the castle like a fog; it was not a living creature, but it fought and struck like an octopus with constantly sprouting tentacles. The sudden unleashed fury about the castle was like a colossal whirlpool, into which were swept Simon and the human form of Mr. Morris, tiny pawns in a ruthless game that had reached its climax. It seemed that there was wrestling and conflict in the skies, and the ground reverberated to the shuddering impact of warring forces.

'Do you think we ought . . . ' It was Denis speaking, but his voice was lost in the thunder, and from his face it was obvious that he had not really known how to finish the question. They were powerless — spectators, nothing more.

Mrs. Morris, in a strangled, pitiful voice, said: 'Rhys . . . '

Denis took her hand and held it firmly.

The fog thickened, as though squeezing the resistance out of the castle. Its lower edges crawled like the drifting ends of a wind-blown curtain. A long, high screaming began at the very summit of the hill, issuing from the fog: it might have been the voice of the hill itself, or the cry of the tortured world, for it certainly came from no human throat.

'I think we ought to move back a bit,' said Frank, trying to sound calm. 'I've got a feeling that there'll be a nasty wrench soon.'

'I can feel something building up,' Denis confirmed. 'But Dad — '

Mrs. Morris said, her mouth trembling: 'There's quite able to look after himself he is. He's out of our care now. Go down the hill we ought — he'd want us to.'

Reluctantly and yet thankfully they turned and went some way down the slope from the house, their way lit by the light that was slowly growing like a flower inside the black cloud hanging over the ruins. Nora looked over her shoulder, and saw that the shape of the ruins was becoming faintly visible. In the smudged outline of the arch was a desperate upheaval, frightening in its ferocity although none of the details were apparent.

Denis said: 'If only we could *do* something . . . '

'Whatever we did,' said Frank, 'it wouldn't count for much either way.'

He still had his arm around Nora. Useless as it might be in the face of the unleashing of such cataclysmic forces as those milling about the castle, it was an undeniable comfort. She smiled at him. Just this reassuring pressure of his arm was more of a solace than all Simon's attempted verbal reassurances. But then, Simon . . .

She turned as they halted, staring up with unwilling fascination into the pulsating cloud. What had happened, or was happening, to Simon and her father? Their weak, human frames were the focal points of the conflict. And Jonathan . . . he had provided the pathway for the old gods. She wondered, shuddering, what hideous death he had suffered at Simon's hands in order to fulfil the conditions of the return.

'It's coming,' said Denis abruptly in a low voice.

The fog lifted as though blown away by a great breath of wind. For one second they saw the slime and putrefaction that rippled back through the gateway, and standing before the arch was a shape of fire, like an angel with a flaming sword; then a great stab of light struck from the heavens and played like water over the ruins, splashing and dancing down the slope and immersing the farmhouse.

Mrs. Morris could not stifle a cry, but it was lost in the last roar of destruction. The castle seemed to rise in the air like a stricken beast, and its dissolving fragments rained upon the hillside, plunging fiery coals into the house, which fell apart. With uncontrollable sensations of regret and yet peace, horror and yet acceptance, Nora saw their home shattered and crumbling.

The light faded as though it had never been, and the noise died away into a faint, musical whisper that shredded away into the morning sky. Dawn stretched sweetly over the earth, and a clean, frosty smell drifted up from the valley.

15

As they approached the blackened heap that had once been the castle ruins, they walked not on snow, but on charred grass and hard earth. The battlefield was uncannily still.

Lying on his back, staring up with sightless eyes at the flushed sky, was Mr. Morris — like a burnt-out fuse, thought Nora.

Denis kept close to his mother. She went without faltering to her husband's body, and knelt down beside it. If tears choked in her throat, she made no sound. His tranquil face, lit with a rapture that had not faded in death, made the thought of weeping seem incredibly foolish.

Denis said: 'It was too much for him — too much for any man. Whatever acted through him wore him out in a wonderful flash.'

'That's why we came to live here,' said his mother. 'Now I see. Driven here, we were — he told me we had to come, and no reason there was for it, but he felt it like that and knew we had to come.'

Nora looked around, but there was no sign of the corpses of Simon and Jonathan. Surely they had not escaped? Then she looked into the small mound that had once been such an impressive ruin, and in her mind's eye she saw the shape of the arch, and bit her lip fiercely; thinking of two human beings, one almost surely dead, the other possibly alive, being dragged in with the retreating spawn of evil.

'Your father was chosen,' said Frank quietly, bringing her back to clean reality. 'Perhaps now, but more likely a long time ago, it was decided that he should be the instrument for the saving of mankind. He might have been a descendant of one of the families of White Adepts, just as Simon was one of the Black Adepts. Or it may have been something slumbering in his mind, ready to be awoken when the time came. Or perhaps it is something that is in the minds of every one of us, waiting for the day when it is needed. We do not all respond to the call when it comes.'

Nora said: 'Father was chosen — '

'Because he was the best of us,' said Denis. 'He was a good man.'

They looked down on that ennobled face.

'Where can we take him?' said Nora.

'No house there is any more for him to lie in,' said her mother.

They stood on the hillside, coming slowly to appreciate the magnitude of their loss. Nora did not feel forsaken, with Frank beside her, but she realised that difficult times lay ahead. He said in a low voice: 'Don't worry: it will work out all right.' She looked up at him gratefully.

'Let him lie until we have been to the village,' said Mrs. Morris with sudden decision.

'But mother, out here — '

'Where else, girl? And what has he to fear now? He is being watched over — as we all are.'

They bowed to her wishes and left Rhys Morris with his face to the heavens.

Nora, conscious of the cold and the

inadequacy of her attire, looked down apprehensively towards the village. People were coming out of their houses and up the slope to investigate the strange phenomena that had brought them from their beds or from their breakfasts. Breakfast . . . the thought of it, with all its everyday associations and the normality it implied, affected Nora more strongly than the sudden realisation of her hunger. The ordinary world, shaken more than anyone down there could realise, was stable and unchanged. In another moment they would be in the middle of it, fussed over, commiserated with in their loss, and subjected to innumerable kindly attentions.

She said: 'What are we going to tell them?'

'That's a thought,' said Denis, halting. 'Who's going to believe the true story?'

'We all know it's true.'

'That won't help,' said Frank. 'It's still incredible. If a dozen people had told me a story like this one a couple of weeks ago, I wouldn't have hesitated in declaring them all insane. No, it's too much to expect them to accept it.'

'So we've got to think up a pack of lies?'

'Whatever we say,' Frank pointed out, 'the scientific know-alls would say that it was all an electrical storm, and that we suffered from mass hallucination. That's reasonable — or that's what they think. Far more reasonable than gods and such wild fantasies.'

Someone shouted up to them. They waved back.

'Well?' said Denis. 'If they're willing to accept an electrical storm, it would certainly dispose of all questions about Brennan, Jonathan and Simon. We can just say they were — well, lost.'

'Don't sound so cold-blooded,' Nora protested.

'We've got to be honest about it. There's going to be an enquiry. Do you want to be grilled as a suspected lunatic — even as a suspected murderer, if we persist in telling improbable yarns — or are you willing to bow to the people who can always pop up with an explanation for weird natural storms and associated phenomena? Mother' — he appealed to her seriously — 'what do you think about it? If you want us to go ahead and tell the truth, we'll do it. It's up to you.'

She shook her head. 'Asking my advice, is it? There's not often you do that, Denis bach. You know best . . . there's right you are, I'm thinkin'. We wouldn't be believed. We know what happened, and it's inside us that we'll remember, and perhaps that is best. Tell them what you like — there's no matter.'

'We can tell them it was something strange we didn't understand,' said Frank. 'We don't know what happened. We were dazed. They can hardly complain about that.'

They looked at one another and accepted this without a word. Then they continued down the hill towards the party of villagers who were coming up. Unthinking, they passed through what had once been a barrier — that impassable force that Jonathan had brought into being to keep them imprisoned and to keep out anyone who might intrude on his schemes: those schemes, thought Nora, that had come to such a shocking end for the warped little man.

The isolation of the weekend was gone. They were surrounded by friendly, questioning faces — faces that became grave when the news of death was told. There was friendship and warmth, and Nora found the assistance that was offered more welcome than she had expected. She felt tired now that the strain of the night was ended, and saw that her mother, too, was pale and haggard. There were friends on all sides: some of them had in the past seemed stupid or uninteresting people, but when they came forward like this in a time of stress she realised how much a part of her world they made up. It was easier and so much more comforting to succumb to their eager attentions.

Mr. Morris was brought reverently from the side of the hill to the village. Of Brennan and the other two there was no trace.

'Burnt up, isn't it?' said many of the villagers who had stood in awe at their windows and watched the incredible lights playing about the castle. 'A storm like that there has never been here before, not in our memory nor the memories of our fathers and grandfathers.'

It was better to leave things that way.

Men went up to study the charred ruins and to make wild guesses. They turned over stones that had been subjected to such an intensity of heat or pressure that they had become mere blocks of compressed powder. And where had the bulk of the ruins gone? The whole affair was fantastic, and only a fantastic explanation would have been truly satisfactory; but the people who could give that explanation knew better than to attempt it.

The books had gone. A blackened leaf drifted down on to the snow every so often, but it was unreadable. There was nothing left of that ancient lore.

Nora, walking with Frank across fields in springtime, when the snow had finally been coaxed away by the warm sunshine, thought sometimes of the books and the adepts who had sought them across the centuries. Perhaps, she thought, there are other copies, and it's only a matter of time before more seekers come to this place and perform their rites before the place where the archway stood. What then? She could not repress a shudder, and Frank would look down at her with concern. 'What's the matter, Nora?'

'Nothing. Just unpleasant memories that pop up every now and then.'

'You must forget them.'

She forgot them ... except for occasional moments of doubt and fear for a future in which the adepts came again, searching for the dark gateway.

In spring and summer the trippers and visitors came and lamented the destruction of the old landmark. The ruins had been so picturesque. They wandered disconsolately over the grass that was already beginning to establish itself over the shattered mound, hiding the last vestiges of the ruins that had been more than an ordinary landmark. The ruins that had been a beckoning, alluring signpost across generations of blackness and evil, were now no more, and in their place the clean breezes played over the grave of Rhys Morris, lying at peace in the unconquered earth.

We do hope that you have enjoyed reading this large print book.

Did you know that all of our titles are available for purchase?

We publish a wide range of high quality large print books including:
Romances, Mysteries, Classics
General Fiction
Non Fiction and Westerns

Special interest titles available in large print are:
The Little Oxford Dictionary
Music Book, Song Book
Hymn Book, Service Book

Also available from us courtesy of Oxford University Press:
Young Readers' Dictionary
(large print edition)
Young Readers' Thesaurus
(large print edition)

For further information or a free brochure, please contact us at:
Ulverscroft Large Print Books Ltd.,
The Green, Bradgate Road, Anstey,
Leicester, LE7 7FU, England.
Tel: (00 44) **0116 236 4325**
Fax: (00 44) **0116 234 0205**

THE HEEL OF ACHILLES

Gerald Verner

*'I'm done for . . . find X.1 . . . Dene
. . . You must . . . Tooth-paste . . . '*
England is at war with Germany and
Dene of the Secret Service tries to
decipher his fatally wounded colleague's
garbled message — potentially vital information for England's survival. Who is
X.1? What does the word *Tooth-paste*
signify? Dene must find out and stop
X.1, or the Third Reich will strike a
crippling blow to England and change
the course of the war. And he has just
eight days in which to do it . . .

DEAD SECRET

Gerald Verner

Criminologist Felix Heron and his wife, Thelma, investigate Sir Percival Trench's death on the hunting field. The inquest's verdict is that it was an accident, but his fiancée thinks otherwise. The case becomes increasingly complex, not least when it appears that Sir Percival's fortune of two hundred and twenty thousand pounds has vanished. Then, when the dead body of a 'grass' is found hanging on a tree — Heron has plenty to work on before finding an unexpected solution.